THE BODY IN THE PERCH POND

An Up North Mystery

By

Douglas Ewan Cameron

Argus Enterprises International, Inc.
New Jersey***North Carolina

The Body in the Perch Pond © 2011.
All rights reserved by
Douglas Ewan Cameron

No part of this book may be reproduced or transmitted in any form or by any means, graphic, electronic, or mechanical, including photocopying, recording, taping, or by any informational storage retrieval system without prior permission in writing from the publisher.

A-Argus Better Book Publishers, LLC

For information:
A-Argus Better Book Publishers, LLC
9001 Ridge Hill Street
Kernersville, North Carolina 27285
www.a-argusbooks.com

ISBN: 978-0-6155767-0-1
ISBN: 0-6155767-0-2

Book Cover designed by Dubya

Printed in the United States of America

Acknowledgements

This book would not have been possible without the help of many people but most especially Douglas Atchison, Sheriff, Alcona County, Michigan, who gave me valuable insight into workings of the sheriff's office. Other people who have aided are Gary Andrew Bokas, Esq., for legal advice; and Bill McClellan who helped with Williston's weapons because I don't own guns. I also want to acknowledge Bob Alvey as the inspiration for Dugal McBruce and in great part the book and Mary von Zittwitz who diligently proofreads all my works. Most importantly I want to thank my wife Nancy Calhoun Cameron for her undying support and encouragement as well as proofreading and criticism.

Hibbard Pond and its environs don't exist – if they did Hubbard Lake where we summer and its environs wouldn't. The people in this book are all from my imagination. However, for those Hubbard Lake friends who read this book and see themselves as one of the characters – if you like the person, it's you and if you don't, it's not.

The story of the loon told by Herbert Smythe is from *Voyage of a Summer Sun – Canoeing the Columbia River* by Robin Cody, published by Adolph A Knopf, New York, 1966.

I must acknowledge two writers who have influenced my work. First (and only chronologically) is Mary Higgins Clark whom I heard speak at a Book and Author Luncheon sponsored by The Plain Dealer of Cleveland OH. She said that many of her works got their genesis with the words "What if." And thus it was with this book as my friend Jerry and I were picking up rocks from the bottom of what would be a perch pond, as did Dugal and his friend Jerry, and wondered, "What if a body was buried in that earthen dam?"

The other writer is the late Philip R. Craig, author of the Martha's Vineyard based J.W. Jackson mysteries. My wife and I met him and his wife Shirley on a riverboat trip from Constanta, Romania to Amsterdam, Netherlands in 2005 and shared many a happy meal together including my wife's birthday dinner. He told me that in his writing, while he knew the story line, he often didn't know how it was going to come out and let the characters lead him. Often that is what I do, and I did in this book.

Dedication

To Nancy Calhoun Cameron, my muse in literature and life.

Prologue

The cold wind whipped the snow in small torrents, dashing it against the ground, the tire, the lantern, his hands, his face – especially the light. Coming in brief gasps the wind caused eddies in the falling snow and whipped what had already fallen back into the air, obscuring his work. If it wasn't the snow obscuring the wheel lugs, it was the snow whirling in front of the lantern's lens and dimming the light. He cursed his luck. He cursed his lack of electronics. He cursed his hands crippled both by arthritis, the cold and old injuries. If he had a radio – a simple radio – in the truck, he would have (could have) heard about the storm. That is, if he had been able to get a signal but this area was so remote that most signals were difficult to get even in the best of times. But it probably wouldn't have mattered. He still had to get her help.

His half-frozen fingers of his left hand could not control the lug wrench adequately and the half-frozen fingers of his right hand couldn't hang on to the lug nut, which dropped into the snow under the tire.

It wasn't the storm really, he knew, as he groped under the tire for the nut. It was really the tire – bald, over used – it had given out as he hit the last pothole. He knew it was there because he drove the road once a week and he had watched it develop through the long winter.

His groping fingers felt the nut – or a pebble – and closed on it. "*Thank goodness,*" he thought. He had already lost two and losing a third would leave him only two on the wheel. In such treacherous weather, two lug nuts holding on the wheel that helped to power the truck would not have been good.

He put what he hoped was the lug nut into his mouth and sucked at it to clean the snow and ice. It was bitterly cold but there was no alternative. As the snow melted his tongue felt the hole in the object and could discern the sharp corners. His luck was beginning to turn. Spitting the nut into his palm, he turned his head, spat the water and remaining debris into the snow. With his other hand, still holding the lug wrench, he wiped the snow off the lantern's lens and then tried to start the nut onto one of the lugs.

He breathed a sigh of relief as the nut caught and he gave it several turns. He fitted the lug wrench to the nut – easier than the nut onto the lug – and started turning it.

"Need any help?"

The voice from nowhere startled him and he dropped the wrench into the snow. Turning to his left he could make out a form behind a bright beam of light. Beyond that were flashing red lights.

"What?" he stammered but "*Cops,*" he thought.

"Didn't mean to startle you," the voice said. "We thought you would have heard us stop. My wife and I are on HPCP" – "Hip-Cip" he pronounced it – "patrol and saw your truck at the side of the road. You should have used a flare and had your flashers on."

His mind raced. Things were cloudy, disconnected. Then something clicked and a semblance of understanding formed.

"No – I'm sorry." His eyes returned to the wheel as his hand retrieved the lug wrench and fitted it once again to the lug. "My flashers don't work and I have no flare – didn't mean to be out in this storm."

"Well, none of us should. Can I give you a hand?"

The Samaritan was now crouching at his side. A red and black jacket, red and black balaclava, making his face indiscernible, topped by a HPCP baseball cap. The man's right hand held a powerful lantern the beam of which he directed at the wheel.

"Just finishing," he responded. "Blew a tire on the chuck hole. Had to get my granddaughter home."

Damn! Shouldn't have said that. Too confused. Too cold. Too many things all at once.

The Samaritan's powerful beam moved from the wheel toward the front of the truck.

"We can take her in our truck if you want."

The Samaritan was up and moving toward the cab.

"No." A final twist and the lug was tight. He stood up and put out a hand to arrest the other's movement. He couldn't take the chance – he couldn't let the Samaritan see her. Even after so long, who knew?

"She's fine. The cab's warm and we'll be on our way in just a minute. Thanks anyway."

"You're certain?" the Samaritan said. It wouldn't be any trouble. We have four wheel drive."

"You're mighty kind," he said. "But with the tire fixed, we'll be fine."

The other retreated and he moved to the back of the truck, inserted the tire iron in the jack and started lowering the car.

"If you certain..." the Samaritan said.

"Yes, thank you," he said wishing the other would leave.

"Alright. Be careful. This storm is supposed to hang around for a while and the roads are icy."

"Right. Thanks. We'll be fine. Her home is very close and I'll stay the night."

"Okay - be careful."

The Samaritan turned and focused his light on his truck parked on the other side of the road and made his way to it and opened the door.

******

John got back into his vehicle, luxuriating in the warmth. Glad to be out of the storm. In his rearview mirror he saw the lights of the truck come on as the exhaust belched a plume of black smoke.

"Is everything alright?" his wife Myrna asked.

"Yeah," John said. "Some old guy blew a tire in a pot hole. Says he's taking his granddaughter home. Must not be from around here. Didn't recognize the truck – an old Ford 150, must be one of the first."

John watched as the other vehicle pulled off the shoulder and disappeared into the blinding snow.

"Should we log it?" Myrna asked as she picked up the microphone to the CB.

"Nah," John said. "We've already clocked out. Herb's probably shut down his base. We need to get home ourselves."

"We should never have gone out," Myrna said. "We knew there was a storm brewing."

"Well, we didn't know it was going to hit here or hit this hard," John responded as he pulled off the shoulder. "Who would have guessed that the storm would hit with this fury when we were completely on the other side of the lake. We should have gotten a room at the Dew Drop anyway instead of coming all the way back."

Some fifteen minutes later and not much more than two miles down the road, his headlights picked up the sign at the end of their driveway and he turned into the protection of the evergreens.

"We're safe now, just a quarter mile to home."

"Thank goodness," Myrna said and they smiled at each other.

******

He was anything but safe as the savage winds of this late winter storm whipped the snow against the windshield and caused the light from the headlights seemingly to flicker in and out of existence. He glanced at the blanket wrapped form on the passenger side. *"How close that was,"* he thought. His eyes moved quickly back to the windshield.

The snow seemed to be coming down harder, his windshield wipers could scarcely keep up with it. He was traveling slowly, not more than ten miles an hour when he hit a second pothole. This one was deep and the front wheel bounced in and out and he wrenched the wheel, trying to keep the rear wheel out but it was to no avail. The turning of the wheel started the truck sliding and the rear wheel plunged in, the torque of the slip whipping it against the outside lip putting such a strain on the three poorly tightened lug nuts that one of them striped almost to the end and the wheel began to wobble.

He managed to get the truck stopped sitting broad side on the road and knew that something had happened to the wheel but he didn't know what. He thought about getting out to look at it but knew that it wouldn't make any difference. He should have let the Samaritan take them … no, that was impossible. The fewer who knew, the better. He checked the form wrapped in the blanket to his right, opening the fold and feeling her forehead. Hot and damp – hotter than before. The fever was getting worse. He had to get help.

Despite its age, the truck had continued running because instinctively he had never removed his foot from the clutch. He oriented himself the best he could, backed the truck up a few feet, turned the wheel and slowly started forward. The knowledge that she needed help – more than he could give – urged him on and once the truck was moving, he started increasing the speed. He could feel the wobble in the rear wheel and knew for certain what had happened. Something bad but there was nothing he could do about it. There was no choice but to continue on his way – she need help, help that he couldn't give her.

He knew that he was coming up to Comrock's Point and its infamous S-curve, called Dead Man's Turn by many of the locals. It had taken several lives over the years. The most recent, two earlier that year when a couple of young men heading home from a night at one of the local bars, had misjudged the turn in the snow and flown thirty or forty feet, smashing into a huge oak that now had two white crosses at its base.

He knew the road even in the whiteout having lived in the area all his life – except for those three years in that godforsaken jungle hell hole. He was getting close and would have to … what was that? Something in the road! Something big! His right foot moved from accelerator to brake as his left foot moved to the clutch. The truck immediately started to skid to the left. Ice! He turned the wheel to the left but no – the skid stopped as he felt the tires get traction and he released the clutch and spun the wheel to the right. Immediately, once again under power, the tires spun, the wobbly one gripping for traction but finding only ice. The truck swung to the right in another skid, he released the brake, cursing himself for his foolish response. Even as he turned the wheel the right rear tire caught another pothole, the poorly fastened lug nuts gave, and the right wheel buckled. The remaining lug nuts stripped and the wheel came off, falling and catching the brake housing and turning into a sled. The skid turned into a sidewise slide taking the truck off the road, across the shoulder – into the nothingness at the south end of Comstock's Curve. The right rear wheel spun, catching only air and swirling show. The truck seemed to teeter momentarily, then disappeared from view.

The sixteen-point stag hadn't moved from its position in the middle of the road since it was first caught in the glare of the truck's headlights. Even the sounds of the final crash as the truck came to its resting place at the bottom of the fifty-foot embankment hadn't bothered it.

Stillness pervaded the air. The snow whipped wildly about the stag as he slowly continued his journey across the road and into the shelter of the woods. Within minutes the winds and snow of the late winter storm had obliterated all signs of the stag and the truck. Nature was in control.

Chapter 1

The hallway was quiet – at least for the moment. A few moments ago it had been ablaze with gunfire, the flashes lighting the place up as through flashes of lightning. He had been lucky and they – at least one of them – unlucky. Viewing the hallway through his night vision glasses the only heat source was about halfway down the hall and against the way where the other had fallen. Its heat signature was orange, yellow, and green but fading quickly as, despite the heat of the area, the heat of life left what now was an empty non-functioning husk.

He had come through the doorway quickly as the area just terminated was becoming extremely hostile from an unexpected crossfire. It had been an ambush cleverly constructed by Them and he led his patrol right into it. When the hostile fire erupted, he leapt into the doorway crashing through the door as though it were paper – none of his patrol had followed. Luckily he had rolled and come to his feet, weapon pointed in front of him at the three forms glowing orange, yellow, and green with no trace of blue and that meant one thing – enemy. He had opened fire instantly speeding his weapon side to side, flashes of red and yellow marking shells exiting and red traces lighting the way.

As quickly as the firefight had started it was over and, for once, he was the last man standing. He was breathing hard, adrenalin coursing through his veins, hands sweaty. He had found refuge, such as it was, in a shallow nook that probably was a doorway but the wall or door was solid as he pressed against it. He watched the heat signature of the one of Them he had nailed fade into cold darkness and all that remained was a dim form.

"What about the other two?" he thought. *"Weren't there three?"* It was times like this that instant replay would be good but that was not real life or at least he had never found the re-wind button.

All was still, there was no sound, nothing moved. Beyond the still form he could see a doorway on either side of the hall. Were the doors open or closed? He couldn't tell but knew he would find out quickly because that was the way he had to continue since going back through the doorway was suicide attested to by the sounds of gunfire behind him. The only way to go was forward and the longer he waited the more time it gave the others to regroup.

He stepped out quickly, weapon at the ready. At the same instant, as though it had been programmed, the two Them stepped out.

"Dugal."

The unexpected call caused him to flinch; he was on target for the first but not for the second and he saw gunfire erupted from the right hand foe and then blackness.

Flaming orange letters appeared on the screen:

> You have been killed by Them
> Too Bad
> Them are deadly
> Do you wish to go back to the last safe spot
> or
> discontinue the game?

"Dugal, if you're going to meet your sportsmen, you better get going."

Earleen's voice shrill because she wanted him to hear from two rooms away cut into his thinking like a sharp knife.

"Gotcha," Dugal responded.

He clicked the discontinue icon knowing that he could restart from last saved game and possibly be more vigilant and avoid the trap this time or perhaps react as before and find out what that hallway had to offer.

"Dugal, did you hear me."

"Yes, I'm logging off."

With a sigh, he moved the mouse cursor to the monitor's upper left hand corner to start the screen saver and clicked on it. To delay much longer would only draw another prompting call from Earleen, this time even more emphatic, not nagging but helpful as he could easily get lost in the game. He swiveled away from the desk and started for the great room.

The aroma of baking bread greeted his nostrils as he crossed through the bedroom, enticing him to hurry. He grabbed his jacket off the back of the door and stepped into the great room, bumping into Earleen. She looked up at him, her green eyes flashing.

"I was just coming to rescue you from the hold of that beast," she said.

He put his arms around her and placed a kiss on her forehead.

"I managed to escape from its grasp by myself – difficult though it was."

"Sometimes I wish that you had never discovered the Web. You pay more attention to that computer than you do to me."

"Sometimes I do – but not always." His hands moved down her back to her buttocks, which he playfully squeezed.

"Not now, you dirty old man. You have your fishing pals waiting." She freed herself from his grasp and headed for the kitchen area. He watched her move through the room, still thrilled by her walk after 35 years.

"Well, maybe later if the beast doesn't snare me again." He said struggling into his windbreaker.

"Oh, get on with your business," Earleen cooed.

"Should be back mid-afternoon according to what Ed said at the meeting last night. Don't know what we're doing for lunch." He opened the door and stepped on to the front porch – well, front porch to Earleen and back porch to him.

The cabin was situated in the middle of a stand of birch, beech and pine with a sprinkling of northern red oak. Thirty feet in front of him he could see the sparkling water of Hibbard Pond as the rays of early morning sun reached it. Wisps of the early morning fog near the shore, the morning warmth having already dissipated most of it. The porch extended some fifteen feet from under the sheltering roof where he stood into a veranda that wrapped around the bedroom wall out of sight.

The setting of the cabin had been the determining factor to them when they bought it six months ago. Snow had then covered the ground and the lake was hidden by ice and snow. The real estate agent, Irene Stockwell, had hired one of the neighborhood teenagers to clear the deck and a path to it from the driveway on the other side of the house. Spruce Drive, as the private road into the small development was called, ran two hundred feet from Hibbard Pond Path through a woods more thickly populated with oaks and maples than the area immediately surrounding the cabin before turning sharply left to parallel the lake and giving access to four more homes. The driveway to their house ran right at the point it turned for one hundred feet. The driveway ended at the garage, detached from the house by some twenty feet.

After parking Dugal and Earleen had their first view of the cabin, smoke gently wafting from the chimney from a fire Irene had lit some half an hour before – she knew how to set up a place to show its best features Dugal thought as he reminisced. He usually did when he stepped out of the cabin into the chill of a late spring morning, the sharp cold bringing back the pleasant sensation of that bright winter morning. The warmth of that fire had certainly been welcome that morning. They had seen the shoveled path leading past the cabin and around to the porch even though there was a door on this side of the cabin.

"I always like to bring people in the front door," Irene had said as they walked down the path single file after coming out to greet them.

"Then why are we coming in the back door," Dugal asked "when the front door is blocked."

Earleen had pushed him in the back. "Knock it off, Dugal," she giggled. "We're buying lake front property not lake back property."

"But you always come to the front of the house first." Dugal had stubbornly maintained and still did since the "back" door entered upon a foyer with a coat closet and stone floor. The "front" door opened into the great room. When guests came in that way, Dugal had to take their coats across the living room area, through the dining area, and hang them in the foyer closet. Still didn't make any sense to him that people coming in the front door hung their coats by the back door.

Chapter 2

Dugal pressed the unlock button on the key fob and Columbus's doors unlocked and the interior light came on. He always parked his Ford Explorer outside the two-car garage as one half of the garage he used as his shop, the cabin not having a basement. Earleen's car, their freezer, and their bicycles occupied the other half.

He backed the SUV out into the small turnout and then drove out the driveway pausing briefly to check for one of his neighbor's cars before turning left onto Spruce Drive. There was no stop sign where Spruce dead-ended into Hibbard Pond Path and the trees extending almost to the road's edge really necessitated stopping even though the Hibbard Pond Path was not heavily traveled. Logging trucks didn't stop quickly enough as they barreled along the road from one of several wooded hunting properties which were being judiciously logged this year.

Dugal lowered his window and waved to Irene who was getting into her car across the road. She worked out of her home that was situated just across the Hibbard Pond Path from Spruce Road and backed up against hundred acres of the best hunting land around the lake. The land had been in Ed Stockwell's family for generations and had included the land upon which Dugal's cabin sat until Ed's father had decided to sell it off to pay off some debts. At that time twenty years ago, the property went for one hundred dollars a front foot and now was twelve hundred dollars a foot as he well knew having brought the property six months before.

He turned left and watched Irene pull out behind him in her white Jeep which she used in good weather having shown them around in her Lexus during the winter. She must do all right, Dugal had mused when he first saw her.

There were four vehicles in the small parking area in front of the Hibbard Pond Outfitters and Dugal recognized several of them from the meeting the night before. He parked Columbus next to a green pickup whose door proclaimed it to be one of several vehicles used by Ed Stockwell who owned Hibbard Pond Outfitters – white lettering stated that the store serviced both fishermen and bow hunters.

Dugal entered the store just as one of the men started one of the stories, which seemed to be the main ingredient in most lake conversations.

"Tim Conrad dies and winds up in hell as most of us knows he will. Shortly after his arrival, the Devil notices that the Tim is not suffering like the rest. He checks the gauges and sees that it's 90 degrees and about 80% humidity. So he goes over to Tim and asks why he's so happy. Tim says, 'I like it here. The weather is just like that when I am out in my fields in Michigan in June.'

"The Devil isn't happy with Tim's answer and decides to get him, so he goes over and turns up the temperature to 100 degrees and the humidity to 90%. Then he goes looking for Tim. He finds him unbuttoning his shirt, just as happy as can be. The Devil quizzes Tim again as to why he's so happy. Tim says, 'This is even better. It's like working out in my corn field in July.'

"The Devil, now upset, decides to really make Tim really suffer. He goes over to the controls and turns the heat up to 120 degrees and the humidity to 100%. He finds Tim taking his shirt off and whistling, even happier than before. The Devil can't figure it out. He asks Tim why he's happy now. Tim replies, 'This is great; it's just like I felt harvesting my corn by hand when I was a young man. Really takes me back to happy times.'

"The Devil says, 'That's it, I'll get this guy!'

"He goes over and turns the temperature down to a freezing 25 degrees below zero. 'Let's see what Tim has to say about THIS.'

"The Devil looks around and finds Tim jumping up and down for joy. The Devil can't believe and asks Tim why he is so happy and Tim responds, 'Well, hell has certainly frozen over which means that the Lions finally won the Super Bowl!!!'"

The story is greeted with the usual laughter and commentary on the teller and central character, who in this case is one of the prominent farmers in the county. There are smiles on almost every face since the season a year before the Lions had not won a single game.

Dugal noted one man sitting by himself was not laughing. He held a Styrofoam cup in his hands and was staring into it as though he was reading tea leaves. The other men, most of whom were also holding Styrofoam cups, were standing around a potbelly stove in the middle of the room. Dugal felt the blazing warmth from the stove as soon as he opened the door. A few of the men glanced his way but then returned to the teller of the story who, at the moment was the center of attention.

"Hey, Dugal, welcome," this came from Ed Stockwell who was standing behind the counter in the back of the room. "Grab youse a cupa and introduce yourself."

Dugal waved in rejoinder and took a cup from a stack on the small table by the door and reached for the coffee pot sitting on top of the stove. He was beaten to the punch by one of the men standing around the stove.

"Rob Macintosh," the man said, as he poured Dugal a cup of coffee. "Hope you drink it black 'cuz Ed doesn't provide any other amenities. That's my brother Roy," Rob indicated with the coffee pot the man standing directly in back of the stove opposite the door.

Dugal could have figured that out because he had seen them at the meeting the night before but since they were identical twins it made it easy. Flaming red hair thinning at the forehead, flashing blue eyes, beards as red as the hair although beginning to show the whiteness of age. The only difference (other than clothing) was that Roy had a full beard and Rob only a mustache and goatee.

"And, yes, before you ask the obvious," Rob continued, "our mother named us after Robert Roy MacGregor."

"Robert Roy ..."

"If you are not up on your Scottish folklore, you wouldn't know," Rob explained. "Rob Roy was a famous Scottish folk hero, a Robin Hood type outlaw usually known simply as Rob Roy."

"I've heard the name before…" Dugal started when Rob continued.

"And no, it was not because of some childhood fantasy of our mother or because we were related but simply because he had red hair and was often called Red MacGregor."

"Make sense to me," Dugal said. "I'm Dugal McBruce."

"I caught the Dugal when Ed called out to you, but don't know a McBruce."

"Well, you probably wouldn't because as far as I know it is a name fabricated by my great grandfather. He fell in love with a lass of a neighboring clan but some kind of family feud prevented their relationship. So, being young and in love, they ran off to Wales and got married before boarding a ship to the new world. They needed a name and didn't want to be found so they chose Bruce of her great-grandmother's maternal great-grandfather and added the prefix just to stay Scottish."

"Interesting. Guess we both related to Scottish outlaws," Rob rejoined and started making the introductions to the other men standing around the stove.

A gust of cold air announced the arrival of other men and Dugal noticed the lone man wave to whoever had come in. A man dressed in a Carhartt jacket and jeans and wearing a nondescript baseball cap walked over to the man and shook his hand.

At this point Dugal was talking to David Jones, a short bald man who looked like he could have been a jockey.

"Who's the fellow over there?" Dugal indicated the man.

"Oh, that's Mr. Warmth."

"Mister …"

"Yeah. Hard worker and a dedicated sportsman but difficult to get to know. If he likes you, he will be your best friend but if he doesn't (which is most people) he will completely ignore you."

"The other guy?"

"Jim Winchell. He and George are best friends for now."

"George?" queried Dugal.

"George Jameson aka Mr. Warmth."

Dugal watched Jim and George head out the door just as Ed announced it was "Time to mount up and head for the pond." Dugal headed for the door and heard Ed call to him. So he stopped and turned back.

"Ride with me, Dugal," Ed said as he switched on the "Closed" sign in the window. "I'll fill you in on the details of this project."

"Sure," Dugal responded. "Always glad to save gas."

Ed locked the door and stuck a sign on it. "Working on the Sportsman Perch Pond. Open as usual tomorrow.

Chapter 3

"Something happened to the perch population of the lake. No one knows what, not even the DNR. There are cycles of fish population we are told, just like cycles of weather and depth of the Great Lakes. For example, a few years ago the lakes were low but they're coming back up now. I have a neighbor who says we are selling water to the southwest and cannot be convinced otherwise."

"You know," Dugal puzzled, "I've been wondering about that big pipe line that runs along I-75 down near Flint."

Ed frowned and looked at Dugal who, unable to keep a straight face, smiled and then both laughed.

"Had me going for a minute, Dugal," Ed said. "Now the organization wanted to do something about this since our primary responsibility is helping the fishery so we asked around and Tim Conrad said we could use his pond as a hatchery. We're getting the perch from a place in southern Michigan who usually provides them to private ponds."

"How many perch?" queried Dugal.

"Over one hundred thousand."

Dugal whistled.

"Sized as they are, they don't take up much space but by the time we harvest them at the end of the summer, they'll be two to three inches long."

"How do we harvest them?" Dugal asked.

"We're going to net them."

"Net them!" Dugal exclaimed. "One hundred thousand baby perch?"

"That's where today's work comes in," Ed said as the truck slowed and he turned on his right turn indicator. "Here's the road to the pond."

Ed turned onto a track indicated by two ruts near a line of pines.

"Tim Conrad volunteered his pond. He built it ten years ago to use as an irrigation source for his corn. Worked well too. The problem is that the only water outlet is overflow. You can see it now, about 11:00."

Dugal looked and saw the sun glinting off windshields of several vehicles still about a quarter of a mile away. Beyond that he could see a broad expanse of sunlit water.

"Big," Dugal said.

"The dam is earthen. Tim built it by broadening and deepening an existing stream. That makes the dam an embankment dam. Had to get DNR (Department of Natural Resources) and DEQ (Department of Environmental Quality) approval though but that didn't prove to be too difficult. But to use it for a breeding pond there has to be a way to draw down the water."

"That's today's job, I take it?"

"Yes, we have already dug a cut through the dam draining the water. Tim used his backhoe over the past month. Today we'll finish that and install two pipes basically forming an L. One will run through the dam and the other from the top down on the waterside of the dam. We had two small I-beams welded inside the vertical pipe to take oak flashboards which will form the dam."

"I think I see that," Dugal said. "You can then draw the water down by removing the boards. But what about the perch?"

"George Jameson is building a cage that will be placed at the end of the drain pipe. As the water is drawn down the perch will gather closer and closer to the dam. When we are ready to harvest we will remove the last couple of boards and collect the perch when they are swept, of necessity, into the wire cage."

"Then we can net them in the cage and transfer them to the lake. Good idea," Dugal said. "I was told about Jameson. Seems a queer duck."

"I saw you talking to Jones. Figure that he told you about Mr. Warmth as Jones calls him."

"Yes," replied Dugal. "A little."

"He wasn't always so solitary. He was an outgoing and outstanding guy until his wife contracted breast cancer around five years ago. She beat it – caught it early – but something snapped in George during the year or so and he withdrew into his shell. Ah, we're here."

Ed parked his truck in line with six other pickups and SUVS.

"One last word about George. He and Jones were good buddies before the medical incident. Hunted and fished together. When George withdrew, Jones was left out, cut off like a diseased appendage. He holds a little bit of a grudge so take what he says about George with a grain of salt."

"I don't form an opinion about something until I have looked at it from several different points of view or sources. Then I usually take a middle ground. There always bias – even in print or on TV. You listen to a story on ABC and then on Fox and you have two different stories. The truth is somewhere in the middle."

"My approached exactly," Ed said. "Let's get our boots on and get to work."

Dugal and Ed got their boots from the bed of the truck and put them on, leaving their shoes in place of the boots. As they headed for the dam, they heard a diesel engine start.

"That'll be Tim's backhoe. He's got a little finishing work to do on the backside of the dam before we can lay the pipes."

Dugal could see two large pipes resting on top of the dam near a cut in the middle. The dam itself had a slight bow and the trench was cut pretty much in the middle. A group of eleven men were gathered near the piles, several still drinking from Styrofoam cups. Dugal noticed that George Jameson and Jim Winchell were apart standing near a set of tanks that Dugal guessed were for welding. As they walked up to the main group, they were greeted with a chorus of hellos.

"For those of you who haven't had the privilege, this is our newest member, Dugal McBruce."

"Hey, Doug," one of the men said. "Welcome to Hibbard Pond Sportsman."

"Thanks," retorted Dugal. "Glad to meet you but please, my name is 'Dugal,' it's Scottish and I am not Doug. That's short for Douglas."

"Gotcha," replied the offender offering a hand. "My name is Jerry Hatchet. You can call me Jerry, or Jer or Hatchet. I don't care. Just don't call me late for happy hour."

That drew a chorus of laughs and, to prove his point, Jerry pulled a flash from his hip pocket, uncapped it, took a swig, and then offered it around. There were no takers.

"Well, let's get at it," Ed said. He waved to Tim Conrad who was sitting on his backhoe at the reservoir base of the dam. Tim waved back and then started lifting the bucket of the backhoe.

"Since you two are new friends," Ed said indicated Jerry and Dugal, "why don't you go down and give Tim a hand finishing the trench."

"Aye, aye, captain," Jerry said and led the way down the embankment, Dugal following closely behind. The early morning dew had left the slope slippery and Dugal almost fell on the way down. He saved himself by reaching out and grabbing Jerry's arm.

"Hey, not so fast," Jerry quipped, "I don't get that friendly on a first date."

By the time they arrived at the bottom of the slope, Tim had already stretched the articulated arm of the backhoe into the trench spanning the width of the dam and was lifting it up. The arm compressed and the bucket rose and started swinging to the right toward Dugal and Jerry. They moved quickly away toward the rear of the backhoe and watched as Tim extended the arm and raised the bucket to empty it. Mud fell from the bucket and plopped into a gooey mess below. Then the arm swung back, extended into the trench and scooped another muddy mass. When the arm compacted and started swinging upward and toward them, Dugal noticed something strange dangling below the bucket. It appeared to be black plastic. After the bucket was emptied, Dugal went to investigate.

There was a piece of black plastic in the mud and, just curious, Dugal pulled it. At first it didn't give so he pulled harder and it came free with such force that a football sized oval object was propelled into Dugal. He stepped back in surprise as the object struck his chest and then fell to the ground.

"You okay, Dugal?" Jerry shouted over the roar of the backhoe's motor.

"Yes, just muddy."

Surprise passed, Dugal nudged the object with his foot. It rolled over and Dugal found himself being stared at by two large holes in what appeared to be a skull.

"Hold it, Tim," Dugal shouted and Tim shut down the backhoe. As he and Jerry hurried toward him, Dugal bent and picked up the object, brushing some of the mud off. What he saw was certainly a skull because what else would have teeth in it. Human teeth at that.

Chapter 4

It was half an hour before the first official vehicle arrived although its approach had been heralded for several minutes by the siren. That had ended evidently when the vehicle turned onto the road to the dam. Since the discovery and subsequent telephoning of authorities via a 911 call using Dugal's cell phone, the men had gathered in one group near one of the two pipes. As soon as Dugal realized what he held was a human skull, he had warned everyone away even though human curiosity about the skull had dictated otherwise. It was George Jameson who took control and convinced the men through logical reasoning that discretion was better than curiosity.

"There can be crime scene contamination here just like on C.S.I.," George had said.

"But there has been no crime," vocalized one of the men.

"Really," George had snarled. "You think a human body ended up buried under the dam naturally? 'Well, I'm ready to die so I think I'll dig a grave under this dam.' Get serious."

Since then the talk had been all speculation about who it was and how it had gotten there. Of course Tim Conrad was the center of the conversation as he had been the one who built the dam and had subsequently uncovered the body.

"If I had buried a body there, do you think I would have uncovered it?" Tim had said at one point.

Dugal had stayed out of the discussion for the most part except to explain how he had discovered the skull. Now he watched as a black SUV, red and blue lights flashing, made its way down the grassy road and parked next to Ed's pickup. At this point conversation stopped and everyone watched the SUV in silent anticipation. It was almost a minute before the driver's door opened and the SUV's single occupant stepped out.

He was a big man, easily six foot eight and weighing three hundred pounds, Dugal guessed. He hadn't seen a man that big for some time other than on the television screen when he was watching football. Wearing a trooper's hat made the man look bigger as he closed the door and started toward the group clustered atop the dam. What surprised Dugal the most about the man was that he was black, African-American, Negro – take your choice of the politically correct term, not that it matters.

The man strode confidently toward the group until he was about twenty feet away and then he stopped and looked down the reservoir side of the dam.

"Is that where it is?" he asked no one in particular.

"Yes, Sheriff," Ed had said. "Dugal here discovered it in the second bucket load …"

"Let's keep the information tight for a few minutes, shall we?" With that he started down the hill.

"We've got some extra boots here," Ed said noticing the sheriff's highly polished boots.

"These will clean up just fine," the sheriff said. At the bottom of the hill, he made his way to the pile of mud Tim had dropped and stopped in front of the skull. He sank to his haunches looking at the skull but not touching it.

"Is this all you found?" he said.

"Yes, sir," Tim said. "Didn't think we should go any further."

"Good thinking, Mr. Conrad. The less contamination the better. Who found the skull?"

"I did, Sheriff," Dugal said. "I pulled that black …"

"Come down here and show me please," the sheriff said, still squatting by the skull.

The crowd parted and Dugal made his way down the hill, careful not to slip as he had before. As he neared the skull, the sheriff stood up and turned to face him stopping him five feet away.

"Can you still throw that inside corner fade route?"

"What," stammered Dugal and then realization struck. "Nat?"

"It's Sheriff Jefferson," said Nathanial Jefferson. "Let's keep it like that, kind of official for now."

"Sure," Dugal said.

"How did you find the skull?"

Dugal explained about seeing the plastic and the subsequent explosion of the skull from its muddy grave.

"So you picked it up and brushed mud off?"

"Yes, I didn't know what it was until then."

"The eyes weren't a giveaway?" asked Nathanial.

"No, I mean, I guess but I wasn't certain."

"Where did the mud go?" responded the sheriff.

"Right under the skull. When I realized what it was, I put it down where it had fallen after hitting me."

"Anyone else touch it?"

"No, the only others down here were Tim because he was running the backhoe and Jerry Hatchet. As soon as we knew what it was, we left the area and I called 911."

"Good thinking. Now go back up to the dam and wait until my deputy arrives, which should only be a few minutes judging by the siren. And don't say anything to anyone. Is that clear?"

Nodding in the affirmative, Dugal walked back up the hill and was barraged with questions that he explained he could not answer. They whispered among themselves as they watched a sheriff's cruiser bounce down the grassy road until it stopped behind the sheriff's SUV. A man got out and hurried toward the top of the dam, where the sheriff greeted him. No one could hear what was said between them but the deputy, which is who it was, seemed a bit chagrined as he turned and hurried back to his vehicle. On the other hand, the sheriff strolled leisurely back to his SUV where he opened the hatch. The deputy leaned into his cruiser and emerged with a clipboard. Then he hurried back to the dam where he faced the group.

"Sheriff Jefferson wants you all to sign your name, address, and phone number and then you can go."

"Can't we stay and watch?" someone asked.

"No. This is a crime scene and the more people move around the more likely it is that someone will possibly cover up some evidence. After you provided the information requested, you are free to go but are not to discuss this with anyone."

"That's not likely to happen," muttered George Jameson.

"Except," said the deputy, "for Dugal McBruce, Tim Conrad, and Jerry Hatchet. The sheriff wants written statements from the three of you before you leave."

"I don't have a car here," Dugal volunteered.

"I'll take you back to the Outfitters," Jerry Hatchet offered.

Chapter 5

He had stood in the woods watching, well back so as not to be seen. Although he had feared this in the back of his mind, he hadn't thought it would ever happen. It was, he thought, one of the freak accidents. He wasn't worried – he had been careful and had left no clues. But one could never be too certain. As he stood there he had, as he occasionally did, a flashback to that terrible day those many years before.

It had not been a good day for him – headaches and flashbacks to Nam and its horrors. She had been almost a woman, at an age when both boys and girls begin to question and rebel. He knew because he had been there and he could still remember questioning his parents and how mad he got when they wouldn't answer or the answer was not what he wanted. Often he would stomp out the door taking his rifle or bow and be gone for days until he felt the need for the warmth of the house and the meager love that they offered him.

But he had been different, he had doted on her, given her everything or at least everything that he could at their place. But she wasn't satisfied. It was probably the TV and what she saw on that one station they could get out of Alpena. She wanted to go to school, she wanted to go shopping, she wanted girl friends, she wanted ... When he couldn't take it anymore he had yelled at her but she hadn't stopped. She had kept nattering at him, nagging like a wife: give me, give me; I want, I want; no fair, no fair. In her frustration she had come at him striking him with her tiny fists. She didn't hurt him, couldn't hurt him but she had pushed him too far and, in his frustration, he had lashed back. Not lashed really but pushed, shoved her away. She had hit the chair, stumbled, fallen backwards and, he realized later, hit her head on the cast iron stove used for heat and cooking in the cabin.

When he had pushed her he had walked out, trying to get away as he had done with his parents and he was gone most of the day but he had gone off hunting before and she had been fine. When he came home the house was silent, the stove cold although, in the warmth of that fall afternoon, it wasn't really needed. But in the house there was a smell, an odor he had noticed upon entering. Fetid, foul, something wrong. And then he had found her, sprawled on the floor, eyes open, unseeing, her body cold, blood pooled around her head. Striking the corner of the stove had cracked her skull, no hole that he could find but certainly enough damage done to kill her.

He had cried for an hour or so he thought. He really didn't keep track of time. He knew that he had to bury her but not here, not with his wife and his Sue Ellen, not this Sue Ellen, she wasn't his. Not really but ... that memory faded, he couldn't pull it back, where she had been, where he had found her, taken her, brought her home. But he knew where he would put her. During his absence that afternoon he had wandered the woods, far beyond his own property and had been drawn by the noise of a machine. He had watched from the woods as the man – a farmer he knew, but not by name – had worked in the area by the creek pushing dirt building a dam. He could tell by what had been done it would be a high dam, ten feet or more and it would take days, even weeks to complete.

He had removed Sue Ellen's clothes, washed her body and wrapped her in the plastic sheeting. Then he had carried her and the shovel through the woods, arriving at the spot from which he had observed the farmer in the late evening's twilight. The machine sat idle, no one was around. In the far distance he could see the twinkle of lights in the man's farmhouse. It was too dark to work anymore, he was done for the day. The farmer was but he wasn't. It had taken him some time to dig the grave, not deep, only a couple of feet, and not big but she wasn't big. He placed her in the grave in a fetal position as she often slept. Here she would sleep undisturbed for eternity, he had thought. He had covered the grave quickly, not pausing to look or weep, crying was past. There was a sense of urgency now. Get her buried, cover her, hide all trace, let her rest in peace, rest with the angels. He wished he could use the machine but he couldn't risk the noise, couldn't be discovered and so it had taken him most of the night to bury and cover her so there was no trace of her being there.

The dimness of early dawn had begun to appear as he wearily left the dam and returned to the woods. He settled himself against the trunk of a large oak ten feet into the woods but from which vantage point he could see the dam and the machine. Then he settled himself to wait.

He woke with a start and took a moment to remember where he was but he was alert just as he had been in Nam. The woods around him was filled with the noise of birds so no one was close but there was another noise and then he realized it was the machine and he had stood up and looked. The farmer was hard at work and, judging from progress, had been for several hours and the height of the sun indicated that, mid-morning he judged. He had been tired and had slept the sleep of the dead since he hadn't been awakened. The farmer had covered the grave area with more dirt and moved further toward the opposite bank. He had not noticed the grave or there would be police here. So he was safe and she was safe.

Or at least he had thought so until now. He watched until it was dark before leaving. They were still working with lights then. He could hear the thunder in the distance, he had known it was going to rain – his joints had told him that – that would stop them, at least for a while. He hadn't been seen – he had been too well camouflaged for that. So well in fact that a huge stag had walked past him to the edge of the woods and out into the open before stopping and staring at the hubbub in the distance. Then he had turned around to enter the woods, stopped, looked straight at him, then over its shoulder at the distant people, snorted, looked at him again, and then walked past him and disappeared into the darkness of the woods.

Chapter 6

"And then, just as everyone else was getting ready to leave, Nathanial came storming up the dam yelling 'Hold on a minute. Hold on a minute.'" Dugal explained to Earleen. They were sitting on their deck late that afternoon, watching the sun starting to set and enjoying a glass of wine on their deck for the first time that spring despite the imminent threat of rain.

"What was that all about?"

"He didn't have the manpower. One guy was off sick, one of the two man forensic team was in court and the two others of the day shift were needed to patrol. The force isn't very big and he was having to call in the second shift but that would take a while."

"So he explains it and says that he wants Tim Conrad, Jerry and me and three others to stay until the deputies arrived."

"So who stayed?"

"Ed Stockwell, George Jamison, and Jim Winchell. Everyone wanted to but he said no – there was enough crime scene contamination as it was."

"Just like CSI," Earleen mused.

"That's what Jerry said," Dugal agreed as he took a sip of wine. "He made us sign a form he wrote swearing 'allegiance and fidelity to the sheriff of Alcona County and promising not to talk to the media or anyone else until given permission.' Ed and Jim were assigned to helping his deputy out at the road with crowd control until his other deputies arrived."

"A crowd?"

"No, actually just the media – all four of them – and some 'ambulance chasers' who had followed the lights and sirens."

"What about Mr. Warmth as you called him?"

"Not me, it's what others call him. He helped Tim Conrad build a cofferdam."

"Cofferdam?" queried Earleen.

"It's a temporary dam to keep water out of its normal channel, in this case the trench through the dam where the body was discovered."

"What did you do?"

"Jerry and I were to aid in the forensic deputy in 'sifting' as he called it until help from State Police Crime Lab in Grayling arrived."

"Sifting?"

"Looking for the rest of the skeleton although it was more like mudding. The forensic guy, Rich Walker, did the actual digging. Jerry would put the bones into boxes. I took pictures with a digital camera."

"That sounds boring."

"It was. I would have rather had Jerry's job. What I found interesting when I started taking pictures was all the deer tracks around."

"Deer tracks."

"Yes, they were huge. Probably just made by one deer."

"Was anything found beside the skeleton?"

"Not while Jerry and I were there. Although…"

"What?"

Dugal smiled.

"Jerry thought he saw someone in the woods. He had been bending over mudding, helping the forensic guy and stood up 'stretching his achin' back' he said, when he said he saw someone standing at the edge of the woods. The woods were about a hundred yards away and are pretty dense."

"Did you see anyone?" Earleen asked.

"Nope and neither did anyone else."

"Now that's a piece of information I should have been told," said a voice from behind them.

Both of them jumped out of their chairs and turned to face the sheriff as he strode confidently across the deck.

"You scared ten years out of me," Earleen gasped, her hand over her heart, "and half a glass of Chateau Cardboard d'Eau down my front."

"Sorry about that, Earleen," Nathanial said. "I just walk quietly."

"A man your size should make a ton of noise," Dugal said "but you always were quick on your feet."

"Had to be to protect that skinny little ass of yours," Nathanial said. "I saved you a hundred times senior year on our way to the state finals."

"Yes, but you couldn't do it the last time when they dumped me before I could throw the inside corner fade to Freddie in the end zone."

"If it hadn't been for me, the entire team would have pounded you into the ground."

Dugal and Nathanial laughed and then, as one, threw their arms around each other.

"Don't squeeze too hard," Earleen said. "We're more fragile now than we were then."

"If I break any bones it will be his," Nathanial said as he enclosed Earleen in his arms.

"Careful you big lug," Earleen said.

"Get you something to drink?" Dugal asked. indicating his wineglass on the table.

"Coffee or water," Nathanial said. "I'm still on duty. Hell, with this job I'm always on duty."

Dugal drew up another chair while Earleen went to get coffee.

Sitting, Nathanial said, "Let's get the official part of this over. I've read your statement and there are a few points that need clarification."

"Okay," Dugal said picking up his glass of wine.

"Wait a minute," Nathanial asserted. "What was that Earleen said she spilled on herself?"

"Chateau Cardboard d'Eau."

"Chateau Cardboard d'Eau. What the hell is that?"

"Box wine – her little joke. You know these five-liter boxes? It's fairly inexpensive and good. Besides neither of us can tell much difference between a bottle of Two Buck Chuck and an expensive wine."

"Two Buck Chuck I've heard about. But back to the questions. You said that the skull was in the middle of the pile, so basically in the middle of the shovel's load. You certain of that?"

Dugal reflected on the scene for a minute.

"As certain as I can be. I remember seeing the piece of black plastic in the middle of the shovel's load and it still showed in the middle of pile when dumped. Why?"

"Was the black plastic sticking in any of the skull's openings?"

"I don't know. I don't think so but then I can't be certain. What's the problem?"

"Off the record," Nathanial said, "there is a hole in the back of the skull."

"What? You mean …"

"It could have been made by the backhoe but if it was in the middle of the scoop then it is doubtful. Also there is not a lot of dirt in the skull so most likely the plastic was wrapped around the skull."

"Did you find anything else?"

"Just most of a skeleton. It's slow work with the mud and no water. We had to bring in a pumper from the north end firehouse and use its water to wash the mud off through screens. We think we have everything. They were just starting to go through the stuff that was from the trench around where the skeleton was. Doubt there is anything there but you never know."

"Any idea about identification?" This came from Earleen who had come back with a tray bearing a cup of coffee for Nathanial and a carafe of wine. She was wearing a different dress.

"Sorry about the dress. Hope the stain comes out," Nathanial proffered.

She put the tray on the small table, Dugal moving his wine glass.

"Oh, it's white wine so no problem. Red causes concern."

She handed Nathanial a coffee mug.

"I'll take your word for it."

"You need anything in that? I forgot to ask."

"Nope. Hot and black. Just like me."

All three laughed.

"You asked about identification. We have no idea – don't even know the sex. The bones have been taken to Wallace Hibbs. I'll stop by in the morning and see what he knows. Probably have to go down state to a forensic pathologist."

He took a sip of coffee.

"Hey, this is great coffee."

"It's my special blend," Dugal stated and smiled.

"So, Nathanial, change of subject. How did you get here?"

"I drove my cruiser."

"No, I mean ..."

"Just kidding. I know what you mean. I had a football scholarship to State."

"I remember," Dugal put in. "Best ever for someone from our school at that time."

"Yep, I was in football heaven. Started the fourth game freshman year. We were playing the Hawkeyes. There was a really big nasty guy on defense. Don't remember his name. Late in the second quarter, he came through on my right and I moved to block him and got sandwiched, one high and one low. The knee shattered. It was reconstructed with a long rehab but the doctor said that it couldn't take another hit so I quit."

Earleen had grimaced at the description of the hit.

"I'm so sorry."

"That's okay. It worked out for me. I left school and applied for a job with the state troopers. Got accepted, went through training and worked on the force for twenty years and took retirement. We moved up here ..."

"Whose we," Earleen asked.

"Oh, yeah. My wife Dawn and our youngest Delilah. We have a son Nathanial who went into the service – Marines. Has done well. Married with two kids. Currently in Afghanistan. Coming home in three weeks. Dawn is counting the days.

"Anyway, there was an opening in the sheriff's department here and I applied for it and got it. We moved up here ten years ago. Last spring the sheriff had a heart attack and as senior officer, I was appointed as temporary sheriff. Guess I'm doing all right as I still have a job."

Dugal opined, "That explains your demeanor at the dam this afternoon."

Nathanial smiled showing teeth ear to ear.

"Yep. I am under constant surveillance. And not just because I'm black."

"Must be tough. There aren't many blacks up here."

"It was tough when we first moved here. No outward animosity but we were the only blacks for five years and I am the only one in law enforcement around here. There were a couple of incidents with belligerent drunks but nothing ever went very far."

"But did the other deputies feel offended when you got the appointment?"

"Maybe but nobody said anything. We have all been working together for the past six years so we know each other well."

"When does the job become permanent?" Earleen asked.

"This fall after the election."

She noticed that he crossed his fingers when he said that.

"You running?"

"Plan to – Dawn is going to run my campaign."

"Anyone going to oppose you?"

"There is a guy who's been running every election but always loses. He was a Detroit cop and retired up here. Runs a fishing charter business out of Harrisville. I think he runs just to shake things up and make it interesting although you can never tell."

"You've got our vote and our support," Dugal chimed in.

"Definitely," Earleen rejoined. "We help any way we can."

"That's great. Thanks even though you don't know if I'm a good cop or a bad cop."

Earleen looked at him in mock horror.

"Bad cop? How can homecoming king senior year be bad cop? Especially with such a good looking homecoming queen."

"Dugal should have been king, you know. He led the team to the best season ever."

"Wait a minute," Dugal jumped in. "I wasn't even nominated."

"True but it should have been you and not me," Nathanial retorted.

"Water over the dam."

"Okay, you know how I got here, so what about you two?"

Dugal looked at Earleen who nodded.

"Two months after graduation, we got married, had to. We were both headed to college but Isabel changed things. I learned to drive semis and started hauling cars for Ford. Did that for thirty-two years until our kids were through college and settled. Worked a few years after that just to put money away.

"We started looking for a place to retire to on a lake five years ago. Found Hibbard Pond last year. This was the fifth place we looked at. We liked it, bought it, sold our place which we had owned free and clear for some time and moved here in March."

"You said kids."

"Yes," Earleen jumped in. "Three girls, Isabel and Jennifer within three years, and Kathleen six years later. She, as Isabel, was a surprise. Isabel and Kathleen are both married. Isabel has given us a grandson and granddaughter, and Kathleen is pregnant with twins believe it or not."

"What about Jennifer?"

"She's a lawyer in Florida. Lives in Miami Beach with her partner."

"Oh," said Nathanial, "I ..."

"No problem. We don't hide it. It's biological and there is nothing that can be done. She discovered herself late in high school, told us and has gone forward strongly. What about Delilah?"

"She's an electrical engineer in Los Angeles. Married with no kids and doesn't plan to have any. Her husband is in the front office of the Dodgers."

Nathanial looked at his watch, finished his coffee, and then stood.

"Hate to drink and run but I want to talk to Jerry about that person he thought he saw and then home for dinner."

Earleen got up and came over and hugged him.

"We're so glad to see you after all these years."

"Same. Sorry the circumstances couldn't be better but that is the breaks."

Nathanial and Dugal shook hands and Nathanial left just as the rain started.

****

"It's a small world," Earleen said.

It was much later, dinner eaten, table cleared, dishes washed, a quiet evening spent watching TV news and Jeopardy, and then to bed after an emotionally exhausting day, at least for Dugal.

"Yes, amazingly small. Even after 30 odd years. To wind up so close to someone you had been so close to."

"What?"

"Well, Nathanial and I were close as teammates for four years could be in a suburban Detroit high school in the early 70s. We weren't pals or anything but teammates are close."

"And you're close now?"

"Well, we are involved in a crime. Both on the same team."

"What team is that?"

"The good guys, of course."

"Wearing white hats and galloping off into the sunset?"

"Of course not. But how strange after thirty odd years to encounter him atop an earthen dam in the middle of nowhere."

"I thought it was at the bottom of the dam."

"Whatever. Still fate is strange."

Earleen rolled over to face him.

Dugal turned on his side facing her.

"Fate or chance?"

"Aren't they the same?"

"I guess. That's one way to look at it."

"Well, let's say chance."

"Earlier today you were ready to take a chance."

She slid her hand down between his legs.

"And now fate has given you a second chance to put up or shut up."

Dugal did both.

Chapter 7

The town of Hibbard Corners got its name more from geography than anything else. Someone made the decision to keep things simple so the road encircling the lake was called Hibbard Pond Path, being at the time essentially that. The town was located at the only intersection and so Hibbard Corners was a natural. When numbering came into being it was realized that twenty-two miles of road would make for some mighty high numbers so the road was divided into four sections: North, East, South and West Hibbard Pond Path with the divisions coming at the four compass divisions. It so happened that from the middle of the lake magnetic north went right through the Corners as the locals call it. The roads were then, clockwise starting at that point with East Hibbard Pond Path, etc. There were no logical dividing landmarks and so signs were posted: End East Hibbard, start South Hibbard, etc. When civilization demanded a southern access route, East Hibbard Pond Path was extended southward to M-72.

The town's business district consisted of four main buildings, only three of which were original. The Hibbard Pond Post Office, a ten-year-old red brick building occupying the northeast corner, was the new building. It faced Grouse Road, which was the northbound continuation of East Hibbard. On the southeast corner was the Hibbard Corners Library housed in a white clapboard building formerly the local grocery store. It faced west on East Hibbard but the four-car parking lot was on the north side off Huron Road, the eastbound continuation of North Hibbard. Across from the library on the southeast corner was the only dual occupancy building. The post office had been housed there before the new building and it had shared the space with Henry's Barbershop, which had continued until Henry's death two years before. Currently Henry's space was being remodeled to house Helen's Hair Quarters (most of the residents were trepidatious about that even though Helen Trumball-Grant had been raised in Hibbard Corners). Helen was recently divorced and had returned to the area six months previously moving in with her widowed mother on Hibbard's south shore. It wasn't the business that bothered people but the name. "Why not Helen's like it had been Henry's for so long." That - like other things - was an indication of the area's reluctance to change and the desire to be isolated and left alone. Newcomers were welcomed as long as they pretty much left the status quo.

Where the post office had been was now occupied by Hibbard Pond General Store, which had moved from across the street when the post office vacated. The space wasn't any bigger but it had a second floor where the owners Gert and Peter Pickard lived. They had purchased the building when the post office moved out and rented space to the barbershop. Being able to live upstairs had eased their financial situation immensely since owning a store in an area that was only fully populated in the warm weather was not easy.

On the northwest corner sat the Hibbard Corners Funeral Home although the building looked like a church. As well it should since thirty years before it had been home to the Hibbard Corners Lutheran Church of the Missouri Synod. An argument about the hiring of a new minister had split the congregation virtually down the center. Neither wanted to stay in the old building and had built new facilities. The Hibbard Pond Lutheran Church five miles west on Whitetail Road and the New Woods Lutheran Church ten miles north on Grouse. Interestingly – to the outsiders at least – each congregation had hired the person to whom they had been so opposed before the split. "Strange are the workings of the Lord" was the usual comment.

The church building had sat unoccupied for five years when Steven Hibbs had paid the back taxes and taken possession, turning the building into its current use. Steven had retired five years ago and the business was now run by his son Wallace. It was into the small parking lot on the north side that Nathanial turned about nine o'clock the next morning.

He finished the last of his third cup of coffee, placed the Eddie Bauer stainless steel mug into the cup holder between the seats and opened the door. The early morning chill had rapidly dissipated and the sun shone forth in its late spring glory. Nathanial proceeded to the front door of the church, which faced Grouse, climbed the four wooden steps and entered through the right hand double door – the left being kept locked until it was needed to be open to admit the egress of a casket.

What was formerly the narthex was now the funeral home's office. A muted brown carpet covered the floor; there was a green leather sofa and two wing chairs in front of Wallace's mahogany desk behind which was his mahogany colored leather swivel chair. Soft music (something classical which Nathanial didn't recognize although he liked some classical but preferred New Age music) was playing through a concealed speaker system. A placard sitting on the desk informed the visitor that the funeral director/mortician was currently in the mortuary and that he/she should announce his/herself on the intercom.

Nathanial pressed the button: "Wallace, its Nathanial."

"Come on down, Sheriff, " boomed the response. "You know the way."

"*All too well,*" Nathanial thought. He had been here when his parents had died having brought them to live with him when he had moved from the city. Also he was present for numerous postmortems of traffic accidents and several suicides.

He proceeded down the hallway in what had been the nave of the church but had been divided into two parts, one for storage and the other for casket display, and into the chapel/viewing room which occupied the front part of the nave and the former sanctuary which now was set up to hold the casket. He turned left, open the wide door and proceeded down the ramp that permitted a casket to be wheeled up or down.

Above the door to the left of the landing was a red light next to a light sign that read "Embalming in progress." The light and the sign were always lit to deter the weak hearted. He opened the door and stepped into a well-lit room. The concrete walls and floor were painted white and seemed to glisten in the fluorescent light. The hum of an exhaust fan was the only sound to be heard other than the hum of the lights. On the metal table in the middle of the room behind the bulk of Wallace Hibbs, Nathanial could see parts of a skeleton. Wallace was a big man, a victim of his parents' genetics. His build reminded Nathanial of a bowling ball or Tweedle Dum and Tweedle Dee from Disney's *Alice in Wonderland*. In fact, he knew that Wallace had been called "Wally the Walrus" in high school. His six foot four frame would have been hard to hide in a crowd, even with a professional football offensive or defensive line where his silhouette would have been out of place.

"Hello, Sheriff." Wallace would have seemed to have eyes in the back of his except for the closed circuit surveillance camera that Nathanial knew about.

"Did you learn anything?" Nathanial asked.

"Too much," Wallace said turning to face him. "And not enough."

Nathanial was shocked by the downcast look on his face. He had been in the room several times with Wallace performing autopsies but he had never seen him so distressed. He knew that Wallace had never handled a potential murder before.

"As far as I can tell, this was a young female, age 10-14, early stages of puberty judging by the pelvic canal. There are no abnormalities – breaks and such – anywhere except on the head. There is the scrape possibly where the trencher picked it up and this."

Wallace turned around and picked up the skull that he then held between them in the light. The skull was positioned so that he was looked at the back of it. On the left side Nathanial could see the gleaming white of the scrape, quite apparent against the dark stain of the skull caused by its long-term contact with the earth. Facing him, in the back of the skull, was a hole about the size of a half dollar, its edges jagged and discolored.

"The pieces were found by the sifting, one or two small ones are missing. It wasn't caused by the backhoe, you can tell by the staining. This young lady died by a blow to the head, which fractured the skull. I would judge that death must have been fairly instantaneous," Wallace said.

"There are no other signs of any trauma. The forensic techs brought the bones here last night when the rain began and we worked a couple of hours putting the skeleton together and we have all the pieces except for a few toe phalanges."

Nathanial then understood that is was the nature of the victim and her death that had impacted Wallace's normal high spirits.

"Do you have any idea when?" Nathanial queried.

"I don't have any forensics training, as you know." Wallace answered. "Judging by the condition of the skeleton – the complete deterioration of the flesh – I would at least ten years but that's a guess. Of course knowing that the dam was constructed ten years ago helps."

He grinned impishly, seemingly back in control.

"I have put in a call to the Blodgett Medical Facility and talked to Dr. Swartz. His first impression backs my guess but he wants to look at it personally. I have made arrangements for transportation by an Alpena funeral home. They'll be here in about an hour."

"You've lived here most of your life, Wallace. You know of any teenage girls missing about ten years ago?"

"I wasn't here at the time being away at school for the most part but mom and dad always kept me informed. Nothing that I know about."

"Well, it's a place to start." said Nathanial. "Send me a copy of your report and your bill."

Chapter 8

"Barbara Ann, I want you to check the records for missing teenagers beginning about ten years ago. Go back another five or so to see what we've got. Wallace is fairly certain that the victim was in the early teens. We'll start with that."

"Right, Nathanial," Barbara Ann replied. "Where are you going to be?"

"I'm going to check around here to see if anyone recalls anything. Might not have been reported. You know how some people are. Check back with you in an hour. I'll have the phone with me."

"Roger," and Barbara Ann cut the connection. Nathanial pressed the END button on his cell phone and put it in its case on his hip. He looked at his watch and realized that although the store was open, the first batch of cookies wouldn't be out for fifteen minutes. He crossed Grouse and entered the post office.

The lobby of the post office contained a copy machine, a rack with assorted priority mail mailers, access to about fifty post office boxes and two mail slots with plastic identification signs designating "Hibbard Corners" and "Out of Town." On a piece of paper taped above them was the printed message: "But feel free to put anything in either of them." "*The mark of an employee who can't understand people who use the post office but can't read,*" Nathanial thought.

He pulled open the door to the service area and held it for Helen Trumball-Grant, dressed in coveralls and a tee shirt with the legend "Hair makes the man" with man crossed out, woman written to the right and also crossed out and "person" written above them.

"Morning, Mrs. T-G" as most people called her.

"Morning, Sheriff," Helen said. "Any more information about the body at the perch pond?"

Even if the information hadn't been on the TV news the night before and front page in The Alpena News, word would have gotten around quickly. In the Hibbard Lake community secrets are only secure with one person and even that would be suspect.

The Alpena News had been sensational in their headline.

HIBBARD POND SPORTSMAN FIND BODY

While working on an earthworks dam on the property of Alcona County farmer Tim Conrad, member of the Hibbard Pond Sportsman, found a skeleton buried at the bottom of the reservoir side of the dam. Acting Sheriff Nathanial Jefferson had little to say about the body. "All that has been found appears to be the skeleton of one person. We will take the remains to Wallace Hibbs but beyond that we do not know very much."

The earthen dam was constructed ten years ago by farmer Tim Conrad to make a reservoir to provide water for his animals and crops. He was helping the sportsmen put in a drain that would facilitate using the pond to raise perch that will be netted and transferred to Hibbard Pond this fall. The sportsmen will plant rye in the bottom of the pond and allow it to fill before 100,000 baby perch are put in to grow throughout the summer.

What appeared in the paper was essentially what Channel 11 news, the local CBS affiliate, had reported the evening before. The press, all four of them, had arrived at the scene within an hour of Nathanial's office receiving the 911 call. By then he had the area fairly well cordoned off and the witnesses sworn to secrecy but in the Hibbard Pond society who knew. There was a picture in the paper of the group of Sportsman standing atop the dam looking at the forensic team working below and Channel 11 had a brief clip of that as well as Nathanial making his brief statement.

"Nothing definite," Nathanial replied, choosing not to divulge any information until it was substantiated by the authorities at State. "You don't happen to know anything about a person missing from the area about ten years ago do you?"

"No, but I wasn't here at the time. I was married and living down below then. I'll talk to mama and see if she remembers though."

"Thank you."

The service area was spanned by a long Formica topped counter in front of a large display board featuring stamps and samples of padded mailers. To the right of the counter was the traditional display of wanted posters.

"Morning, Owen." Nathanial said. "Literacy rate up any?"

Owen Whitehawk scowled.

"You'd think that people who could write could read. How do they know what their friends say?"

Nathanial had guessed that Owen was the source of the notice above the letter slots. He had been postmaster for the ten years the new post office building had been open, and a letter carrier for twelve years before that. A Chippewa Indian who had grown up in the area, Owen had joined the USPS after a four-year stint with the Navy after graduating from Alcona Community High School which served the entire county.

"Wallace come up with anything else about the little girl?"

"How did..." he started and then stopped.

Owen and Wallace were close friends having gone to high school together and banded together against their common foes: ignorant teenagers who ridiculed anyone different. Times had changed and Owen's youngest son was the school hero having quarterbacked the football team to the semifinals of the state championship the previous fall.

"No, and I don't want word to get out." Nathanial replied.

"No one will hear it from me, not even Rachel."

Owen's wife Rachel was still pretty enough after five children to be the model she had been until she married Owen and they started their family.

"Do you recall hearing about any runaways from here or in the area about ten or twelve years ago?"

"No, at least not that remained so. Linda Thornton ran away for a while eleven years ago but came back six months later. Rumors always said that she was pregnant and went to live in a home and gave the kid up for adoption. She married Clyde Turner five years ago and moved to Bay City with him. Clyde is a computer repairperson who travels the state for a warranty company. He had been in the TV repair business but got hooked on computers."

The post office and general store were the centers of the Hibbard Pond rumor mill and anything that had happened Nathanial knew he would find one in one place or the other.

"Well, let me know if you remember anything else." Nathanial said and turned to leave.

"You could always ask Gert – if you've got the time." was Owen's parting shot. Nathanial waved.

Chapter 9

The smell of Lemon Crisps wafted out to greet Nathanial as he entered the store. The bell jingled and Gert stuck her head out of the back room. "Be right wit' youse, Nathanial"

Moments later she came to the counter bearing a plate of Lemon Crisps in one hand and a mug of hot coffee in the other.

"Seen youse going into the post office after visiting with Wallace and knew youse'd be here soon. First batch fresh out of the oven."

Thursday was always Lemon Crisps day and unless there was something that really demanded his attention, Nathanial would always stop in about the time the first batch was ready. Monday was blueberry muffins, Tuesday fudge brownies, Wednesday oatmeal cookies, Thursday Lemon Crisps, Friday corn muffins, Saturday depended on Gert's mood although ginger snaps more often than not and Sunday she rested just as the Lord had, she explained. When they had remodeled the post office into the store, Peter had added a small kitchen to accommodate Gert's need to bake. She had always done the baking at home before but the fresh baked cookies quickly became the store's drawing card. Nathanial was surprised that neither Gert nor Peter showed the results of the baking. Both were less than five feet in height and neither topped 100 pounds. They had been married thirty-three childless years though not by choice and were as youthful and vigorous as they had been when they were married.

"Peter's gone to town to take care of some tax business wit' the Secretary of State. Apparently some of the paperwork got misplaced. Youse'd think that in this age of computers, stuff would run more efficiently. Never had any problem with paper."

Gert and Peter were notoriously computer illiterate and intended to remain blissfully so. Their cash register was the old mechanical kind and they did their accounts using an old tape-adding machine.

"Smelling mighty good this morning, Gert. Must have done something extra special."

Gert waved toward the front window in response to the voice coming out of the CB scanner behind the counter. Nathanial turned to see George Haversack's Chevy Blazer topped by the traditional K40 antenna favored by members of the Hibbard Pond Citizen Patrol. George was a retired history professor from a small Ohio college and ran the library, which was open many more hours than it needed to be but gave George something to do in his retirement. His wife Lisa had died two years before from ovarian cancer, just two years after they moved here upon his retirement. She had grown up in Alpena on Lake Huron and they had come back to the area wanting to stay in the north for the change of seasons.

"George always lets us know when he arrives and leaves," Gert said to Nathanial. "He is so lonely without Lisa. He'll be over at lunchtime for two-dozen cookies. Leaves them on a plate on the desk for the kids who come in the afternoons."

"Guess I'll have to stop in for the free cookies." Nathanial said as he took two from the plate and a sip of the coffee.

"Free cookies are always here for youse – and I serve coffee."

"Changing the subject – since I am on duty – you and Peter have lived here quite a while, haven't you?"

"All our lives. Met in elementary school, dated all through high school – except for a brief flirtation with another girl, him not me – and married two weeks after graduation.

"We've lived in two homes, this being the second." Gert continued. "Haven't left much either always been busy with the store and youse can't go off and leave folks without food.

"You're going to ask me something about the body, ain't youse?"

"Yep!" answered Nathanial through a mouthful of lemon crisp. "Every know of anyone gone missing around here?"

"Just Linda Thornton – but I guess youse learned as much from Owen. He always gets the story wrong – told youse something about an illegitimate baby, didn't he?"

Nathanial nodded.

"Well, that's not the case. She went off with a boy from Flint who was passing through on his motorcycle. She was hit real hard and went with him. Didn't work out though – he dumped her after a month and it took her a while to get the courage up to come back. The courage was only needed by her – her parents were very forgiving. Never said a word and treated her like she had never been gone. The rumors were rampant, of course. Youse don't want anybody around here to know what youse're doing, pull the curtains. They'll say something anyway. Hard to hide anything here – you'd think that maybe in the winter when there are fewer people around it would be different. Isn't though, just works slower. Everyone knew about the body in just under three hours yesterday. Those calls going out on the CBs are picked up by more than Peter and I."

She indicated the scanner behind her.

"Must be at least thirty of these around the lake. People use them almost like radio newscast. Youse want to find out what's going on – just listen for a bit and youse'll know."

"Well..." was all Nathanial could get in.

"Have had a lot of passers-through though. Like the kid on the Harley that Linda fixed up with. Don't get many hitchhikers around though with no main roads going through. Nearest state highway is ten miles east, runs up the lake or about five miles inland. Seen some hitchers there some times but not often. Get people on bikes passing though, mostly young folks out to see the country during the good weather. Not like our five compadres though who tend to go on bike tours of the UP in the fall when the colors are out. More likely have poorer weather then. Course its cooler."

She was going about business as she talked straightening things and not really paying much attention. Nathanial thought that maybe the only reason she and Peter have lasted so long was that he couldn't get more than one word in at a time. He picked up a couple of Lemon Crisps and headed for the door waving as he went. He met George Haversack as he closed the door.

"She'll be in the middle of something – got her going and couldn't get her stopped." Nathanial warned.

George laughed. "The creator left out any kind of a stop button with her. She probably won't even know I'm there."

Nathanial wasn't surprised that George didn't ask about the body. George didn't pry much since Lisa died. He was pretty much a loner when he wasn't at the library except for help with the HPCP for which he ran base one night a week and patrolled with who ever needed a rider at least once a week. Didn't seem to be much interested in nature or socializing. *"That must have been Lisa who instigated the prying,"* Nathanial thought. *"Too bad I didn't know her better."*

When Nathanial reached the parking lot behind the funeral home, the hearse from a firm in Alpena was already there and the door to the lower level was open. As he opened his car door, two men carrying a casket between them came up the steps followed by Wallace.

"They made good time." Nathanial commented.

"I had just gotten her into the body bag and was putting it into the coffin when they arrived. I could have sent her in the bag but – somehow it just didn't seem right to travel so informally after all those years under the pond." Wallace explained. "It's the casket I use for lying in state if there is to be a cremation. Been using it for years. No sense in burning a good mahogany coffin."

"What's this going to cost the taxpayers?" Nathanial asked.

"Oh, that's the beauty of it. They were getting ready to go to Ann Arbor to pick up a body and will only charge $10 for the side trip to Grand Rapids. Otherwise, it would have been $500."

"Let's arrange for another body when she's ready to come back – if she does come back." Nathanial said.

"Only if it's by natural causes," Wallace said. "Do not want to handle another like this anytime soon."

"I wonder who she was," Wallace mused.

"That's just one of the many questions I have," Nathanial said.

Nathanial talked to the two men from the Alpena funeral home who then shut the doors and the ambulance pulled out. Walking to his cruiser, Nathanial got in and called Mitchell Webster.

"Meet you at East Hibbard Pond and M-72. You stay with them to Grand Rapids and then return. We're on our way."

Chapter 10

"Remind me again," Jerry said as he bent over and picked up two baseball sized stones, "why we are picking up stones and throwing them into the bed of a trailer pulled by Tim Conrad's tractor, in what is going to be the bottom of a pond?"

It was a week after the body was discovered and the Hibbard Pond Sportsman Association was once again at work on the future perch pond. A work force of twice that the previous week because of the curiosity factor was at work and Dugal and Jerry had been assigned along with eight others to pick up the big rocks on the bottom of the pond. The work had been further delayed a day or two of because rain and the ground was muddy. The stream that made the pond was running and a small cofferdam had been built to permit the installation of the drainpipes. Behind the dam a small pond was forming.

As they worked they had told each other their life stories – there hadn't been time nor had it been appropriate when they were working to recover the bones. Jerry had been an autoworker in several different Ford plants for thirty years and took retirement when offered. He and Liz, his second wife after a young disastrous first marriage, had two sons, one unwed worked for Ford and the other, on his third marriage, was a Flint police officer. Both had completed high school, Liz Community College, and Liz had worked before children and when the two of them were in school full time. "She's the boss, ain't no doubt about it," Jerry said about her. "She lets me have my fun, fishing and hunting, but boy, the foot goes down when I stray a little." Despite his complaining, Dugal had the feeling he didn't really mind.

"Because," Dugal said as he stopped to pick up a football sized rock, "Tim is going to try to till the ground before seeding it with rye and big stones would dull or possibly ruin the tiller blades. Dry weather is predicted for the next couple of days and he hopes to be able to get it done before more rain which will help fill the pond."

"I know but there are times," Jerry said as he crouched and started pulling at a big rock, "that it seems pretty stupid. Hey, give me a hand with this."

Dugal stepped to the trailer and picked up a five-foot long iron bar pointed at one end. He wedged the pointed end into the ground next to the stone and pried. The stone moved a little.

"How about some bulk here," he said to Jerry. Basically the same height at about six feet, Jerry topped 250 pounds, easily fifty more than Dugal.

The two of them applied their strength and weight and the stone slowly came free. Dugal put the bar back in the trailer and they joined forces again to lift the stone and heave it into the trailer.

"What was that?" Jerry said. "Kill the motor, Davey."

David Johns, driving the tractor, turned the switch and the motor died. They stood still and listened.

Faintly they heard "Allee allee outs in free."

They look toward the dam that was over a hundred yards away and saw Ed Stockwell waving his arms and motioning them to come in. Standing next to him was the obvious bulk of Nathanial Jefferson.

"Can't get through a pond day without law enforcement coming," Jerry Hatchet said.

They called to the rest of the stone gathering crew to be certain that all heard and headed back to the dam. It took about ten minutes for all to be assembled around Ed Stockwell and the sheriff.

"Sorry to interrupt your work," Nathanial said to murmurs of pleasure at the break.

"This morning I heard from the forensics lab at state …"

Murmurs of anticipation and wonder.

"… but they don't add much …"

Murmurs of disappointment.

"… beyond what we already know. Since the body was found here by some of you and this will all be in the news by tonight, I thought I would let you be the first to know. I am holding a press conference in Harrisville this afternoon.

"The body, or skeleton really, is that of a preteen or early teen girl. She apparently died by a blow to the back of the head by an object and person unknown. That's not much to go on but the lab did some modeling and have what they think is a reasonable representation of her face. The hair length is that which was fashionable with girls of that age about ten years ago.

"I have some copies of the face and a description of her height and weight which is all we have to go on. The body was free from any breaks and the teeth were basically cavity free – by that I mean there are no fillings – so dental records don't give us much to go on. We will try to flood the media with the pictures to see if they do any good."

He handed a sheath of paper to Ed Stockwell who took a piece and passed them around. The picture showed an attractive girl but nobody recognized her.

"As far as we know," Nathanial continued, "there were no young girls missing in this area in the time around when we assume the body was buried so we don't expect much help here but maybe elsewhere in the state. They have a DNA sample and will run it and try to compare to all databases. Right now that looks like our only hope.

"Any questions?"

There were none and so the sheriff took his leave.

"You have to wonder why someone would bury a young girl where he did," Jerry said as they walked back toward the tractor.

Dugal stopped and Jerry stopped also.

"Did you really see someone in the woods that day?" Dugal asked.

"Sheriff Jefferson asked me the same thing. He had talked to me late afternoon that day and asked me if I had seen anyone. I told him that I thought I did. He asked why I didn't put it in my statement the day before and I said that I wasn't certain and that no one else had seen it. He told me that in a murder case or in a case of suspected murder everything is important."

"If you saw someone maybe he heard we would be working or he heard us working and came to see. Who owns those woods?"

"I asked Tim that day before we left and he said he owns a couple of acres but several different other properties abutted it."

"Well, something for the sheriff to keep in mind and I am certain that he will," said Dugal. "Now let's get these rocks picked up.

Work went on well into the afternoon with a break at 1:00 for lunch supplied by the Loon Creek Inn and Hibbard Pond General Store. The morning session had found the rock cleanup complete and so Tim Conrad set about tilling the bottom. The outlet pipe was in place and so the crew turned to filling the trench with help of Tim's backhoe run by George Jameson, a virtual jack-of-all-trades, Dugal was beginning to realize. Friendly or not, he was a good man to have around. By four o'clock the earth had been moved back into the trench covering the outlet pipe and its vertical access. Everything was tamped down and in place. There was a brief break while Tim spread the seed and then it was time to set the boards.

The oak boards were two inches thick, three feet long and twelve inches high. The top and bottom edges were beveled to ensure a smooth fit. On the back of each board was an eyebolt that enabled a piece of rebar with a L-bend at one end to fit in. This was to help lower the pieces in place as well as pull them out when the pond was ready to be drained.

Rob Macintosh climbed down an extension ladder that was placed on the downstream side of the access pipe. When he was at the bottom, Roy and George fitted the first piece into the slots and lowered it down. There was a muddy clunk as it settled into place. Rob was about to stomp on it when George stopped him.

"The weight of the other boards will set it. Stomping might damage the fit."

"Understood," replied Rob, "send down the next one."

By the time the second plank was in place, water was already starting to back up. The guillotine gate installation proceeded smoothly and quite a pond had begun to grow by the time they were finished. Tim Conrad watched it with satisfaction.

"In about a week, this should be two-thirds to three quarters full. That should be plenty good to put the perch fry in."

Everyone cheered, cleaned up their tools and other debris and then headed home. Everyone but Tim and Ed Stockwell who stood on the dam watching the pond grow and sharing celebratory cigars.

Chapter 11

"Hibbard Pond Citizens Patrol got started about fifteen years ago," John Lloyd was explaining to the McBruces. They were all in Columbus, Dugal driving, John riding shotgun and Earleen and Myrna in the back seat. It was just a week after the perch pond dam had been installed and Dugal and Earleen had accepted the invitation to see what the citizens' patrol was all about. They had picked up John and Myrna at their place at 11:00 p.m. and were learning the ins and outs of the system.

"There had been a series of break-ins at weekenders' homes, that's what the locals call the people who only use their places during the summer on the weekends. The sheriff's department was hard pressed to patrol our area and the rest of the county so a couple of former policemen (two from Detroit and one from Flint if it matters) got the idea of patrolling themselves. They got a CB base station and a couple of CBs and started patrolling. Each patrol vehicle (only one per night) has a CB and talks to the base via Channel 9 so that the sheriff's patrol can hear what's going on. The patrol vehicle (yours tonight) calls in every twenty minutes giving its location."

"But other people could listen in," Earleen said. "Like potential robbers. They would know where the patrol is and schedule their break-ins or time of the break-in accordingly."

"They thought of that," John explained. "They made ten different maps with call-in locations marked. Each location was assigned a number – the same number on all the maps but a different location on each map. Like on map one, 2432 could be the Loon Creek Inn but on map two it is Comrock S-curve. The base decides which map to use on a given night and that information is given to the patrol via telephone before the patrol starts."

"Speaking of reporting in, it's 11:20 so shouldn't we make a report?" Dugal said.

"Right." John picked up the microphone of the CB he had brought and plugged into one of the 12-volt outlets in Columbus. "CP base, this is patrol."

The CB speaker crackled to life "CP base here, go ahead patrol."

John responded, "Current location is" he looked at the map using a flashlight, "1824."

"Roger, patrol, location 1824 noted."

"All is quiet. Patrol out."

"Roger that. Base out."

"Base tonight is Ed Stockwell," John said.

"Wow, he's a busy man," Dugal said. "Runs Hibbard Pond Outfitters, president of the Sportsman, and base for Hic-cup."

"Hic-cup?" queried Earleen.

John laughed.

"You must have picked that up somewhere," he said to Dugal.

"Yes, Jerry Hatchet. He said that the locals refer to the Citizens Patrol as Hic-Cup rather than Hip-Cip."

"Yes, they love to make fun of the flatlanders or downstaters as they refer to those of us who weren't raised here. They feel that we are moving in and taking over, ruining the quiet life they had."

"Is that why there aren't any local residents in either of the organizations," Dugal asked. "I'm just assuming that there aren't any in Hic – excuse me – Hip-Cip."

John smiled.

"Either one is fine with us. Hic-Cup is almost a term of endearment. Which brings up a change of subject or a little since we were talking about names. When we were talking about you going on patrol with us, you said you'd drive, as Columbus was big enough. I take it that your Explorer is Columbus?"

"Oh," injected Earleen. "He names everything. We have two mallards that feed under our birdfeeders and he calls them Rachel and Galahad."

"Because those are their names," said Dugal defensively. "I don't name things. Things have names just as people do. Take for example, the musical *Cats,* which is based on *Old*

Possum's Book of Practical Cats by T. S. Eliot. All the cats had names."

"But he made them up," Myrna said.

"Did he?" Dugal asked.

"Okay, okay," John said. "Sorry I asked but get back to the organization's name. We think if they make fun of us we must be doing something right. You are correct. There is only one local in Hip-Cip. He's an old timer named Maurice Logan."

"Isn't he like the unofficial lake historian," Earleen chimed in.

"Yes," spoke up Myrna who had been strangely and unusually quiet, John thought.

"He was born in what is now the Loon Creek Inn and lived there until he joined the Navy during the Korean War. He qualified for OCS (Officer Candidate School) and graduated at the top of his class, he flew jets during the conflict."

"Flew jets!" ejaculated John, "He was an ace."

"You tell it your way, I'll tell it mine," retorted Myrna.

Turning to Earleen, she continued, "He's always this way. He was a high school teacher."

She held her hand up to forestall further interruption from John.

"We both were. He taught mathematics and English and has to have everything letter perfect. Always."

She paused and added, smiling almost intimately and (if it hadn't been dark) Earleen would have seen a slight blush, "Well, almost always."

"Anyway, back to Maurice. After Korea, he returned here and worked for Lafarge in Alpena until he retired. He has a little place on the lake on the west side. Some say, and I cannot confirm or deny, that he is writing a history of the lake."

Turning to John, she said, "There, is that complete enough?"

"Yes, dear," John said.

"John," questioned Earleen, "Getting back to your history of Hic-Cup ..." Turning to Myrna, she said, "I like that better ... were the robberies every solved?"

"What?" said John, "Robberies?"

"Yes, the ones that started Hic-Cup."

"Oh, yes. In fact, in the third week of patrols, suspicious activity was spotted at a house not far from yours. The sheriff was called and the patrol managed to nab two teenagers leaving the house with a carload of stuff. It was their second break-in of the evening."

Dugal slowed the car and pointed ahead.

"Where's that road go? Is it one we take?"

"No, that's private. It's what we call the Williston Refuge."

"Is it a hunting club?" Earleen wanted to know.

"No, it's about two hundred acres of wilderness. A family name Williston used to live there but they're gone. For some time now," Myrna answered.

"They had a son who, according to local lore, has a place in there. Big log cabin with electricity and everything."

"He is something of a recluse," John added. "People hardly ever see him but there are reports of sightings. The local wags will pass the word around–they call him 'Weird Willie'." And to Dugal, "just make a note in your mind not to drive in there. You can get about fifty feet and then there is a gate and fence that runs at least along the property line paralleling the road. Well, not paralleling because the road isn't straight, but running along the road fifty to a hundred feet back."

"Mister Precise again," Myrna said.

"Speaking of the side roads we drive into, people could think we are trouble coming as late at night as it is."

John laughed. "They used to. About five years ago, Rob and Roy McIntosh were coming out of a road and a sheriff's cruiser blocked them. Made them get out of the car and assume the position. You know, arms on the car, legs spread. It took a bit of talking to convince the deputy who they were."

"Does that explain the pizza delivery sign we put on the roof?" queried Dugal. "I've been meaning to asked about it."

"Yep," replied John. "We used to have magnetic signs for the doors of the patrol vehicle but they fell off often enough. One had fallen off the driver's door that night. Of course, they don't help when you're on a dark road. So, we got a grant and bought five of these so now the locals can look out the window and say, 'Hey, Maude, did you order pizza?' "

Chapter 12

She was gone. So young, so beautiful. First her mother and now her. He had tried too hard to raise her and protect her. It hadn't been easy but she was a good child. He hadn't known how to raise a child must less a girl.

He hadn't known much about girls until he met her mother. That seemed so long ago. Growing up he had been a loner, raised by parents who really didn't seem to care. No, that wasn't true. They did care – at least they took care of his physical needs with food, clothes, and shelter. But they hadn't cared about him – his inner self. No brothers or sisters, a late in life unexpected blessing – no, not a blessing. A curse! No, not a curse either. More of a burden to be accepted. An obligation to be handled.

In high school he had been a loner by choice. Some might have termed him a social outcast – but he wasn't. The other kids (only four hundred in the school) seemed to accept him - at least they tolerated him. He was never made to feel unwanted – but he wasn't made to feel wanted either. They talked to him when necessary; he was welcome at their tables in the lunchroom.

The kids on the bus greeted him – at least they acknowledged him. He was first on the bus in the morning and the last off in the afternoon. He sat in the back, in a corner. Usually the other kids sat in the front and filled in toward the back so the kids who were near him were on the bus the shortest time. He was only over an hour, being picked up about seven and dropped off about five. On days he missed the bus he didn't go to school since it was over 20 miles away.

He lived at the edge of the county and the high school was on the other side. The school in the next county was only a mile away and it would have been easier to go there. However the school district wouldn't permit it.

He never attended sporting events - never had an interest in sports. Really never had an interest in anything except the out of doors. His folks had a big place – and land, over two hundred acres that they really didn't use. He spent his youth roaming the woods in all kinds of weather.

What he knew of nature he learned from nature. He learned to live off the land by watching the animals. He hunted but never killed – then. He had the equipment – the best bow and equipment which money could buy. And he knew how to use it. But then he had no need to kill. His parents wouldn't have accepted the food. Theirs came packaged from the store.

He could catch the fish that lived in the streams that ran through the property. He could have had the best tackle money could buy but preferred a simple hand held line and natural bait found along the banks. He never kept what he caught – then. But he never would have come home empty handled either.

He didn't struggle with his schoolwork – he was smart, he knew, but there was no reason to over achieve that he could see. He managed to cruise along on the borderline doing only what he needed to pass. He knew he had to get through school and wanted just to do that. His parents wanted him to go to college – to learn about business so that he could succeed in life. But by the time he was in school he already knew what he needed to know. They didn't understand and after the first two years of high school had given up.

During the spring of his senior year, he decided that he was going to join the Army. Get away for a while and see what the world was like. Didn't tell his parents. Two weeks after graduation he reported for indoctrination. He didn't have any problem with boot camp and tolerated the discipline. He didn't over impress and didn't make any waves. To all appearances, his Vietnam tour went smoothly. But for him it didn't – the violence and destruction still came back to him in his nightmares. He pulled further within himself.

Two years into his tour, a fire destroyed his parents' house and their lives. They were his only family. What would have devastated a normal person rolled past him like water off a duck's back. When his tour was over he was given an honorable discharge and went home – to the woods. He built a log cabin in the middle of the two hundred acres and lived in it alone for two years.

Then some legal technicalities with the trust left him by his parents took him to Detroit to see the lawyer. He stayed in a motel in a shabbier part of the city because it was cheaper and ate his meals at a neighborhood diner. It was there he met her. She was working as a waitress. Like him, she was a loner but in a big city she had no woods to occupy her and books had become her haven. After high school she had moved out of her parent's house into a one-room apartment in an old tenement. She waited tables to make ends meet but other than that there was only her books.

He had bumped into her as he was leaving after lunch that first day, she was coming into work. He mumbled an apology and their eyes met. Strange how things like that happen. Within her eyes he saw a companion soul. After several seconds she had broken the gaze and gone into the diner. He stood gazing after her until a couple had tried to enter and he was blocking the door. He came back for dinner and she waited on him. Their casual conversation "I'm Sue Ellen, your server. You're new here, aren't ya." for starters deepened and he had hung around outside waiting for her. He had known that he shouldn't just follow her and therefore had approached her immediately. They had walked for several hours talking. She was fascinated with the details of his life in the woods.

They talked again the next night and he had asked her if she wanted to go back with him. She answered yes without hesitation. The next morning they left Detroit notifying only her employer that she was quitting and her parents that she was leaving. She left no forwarding address and never contacted her parents again.

Their lack of practical experience with life and its problems showed itself immediately with her pregnancy. Their desire to be alone was aided by her book knowledge and the ten cartons of books she had brought with her. He alone went out to buy needed supplies and that was seldom. They had studied the medical books together and had watched enough medical shows to have an idea what to expect when she went into labor. Although isolated they weren't out of touch. When he built the cabin, he had installed a generator to provide power for the cabin and the well pump to supply water. She had brought a TV with her and they could receive 3 channels including PBS.

They had discussed the delivery over and over again. The cleaning of the baby, the severing and tying of the umbilical cord. They were as ready as they could be. But the reality of life reared its heavy hand. The delivery itself was simple enough although the twelve hours of hard labor took its toll. Their daughter was a beauty with flaming red hair like her mother and what would become pale green eyes. But inside the mother, something had gone wrong. Something had ruptured and the bleeding wouldn't stop. They knew there would be bleeding but initially thought nothing about it. The realization that something was drastically wrong came too late. He had woken up early in the second morning of his daughter's life to discover his Sue Ellen had died silently in her sleep.

He had never been so alone as he was then. His one brief high in life was followed by a sudden low. A desolation so great that he felt that he would follow her rude exit from this existence. His despondency was broken by the shrill crying of their daughter. As quickly as he had gone into depression he was brought back by the realization that *their* daughter – *their* life needed him to survive. In that small life was all that remained of Sue Ellen and it was up to him to preserve it.

Now that life was gone too. Five years of caring, loving as he had never been loved. Teaching and guiding. The sudden attack of late season flu – it must have been. It had been in the news. An epidemic they had said. He had done his best but it hadn't been good enough. Didn't know how she got it, possibly on their last outing to civilization for needed supplies. She was so weak her fever so high and no matter what he had done he couldn't break it. Finally he had realized that she wasn't going to survive unless he broke his creed and got help. If he didn't she wouldn't make it. He would have to get her to the hospital in Alpena. He had bundled her warmly and they had set off in his truck into the blinding storm that had hit the region so suddenly.

He sat in his chair staring at the TV screen unseeingly as he often did since her death. The pictures were just distant images, vague impressions on his mind.

She was there. He bolted upright and stared unbelievably at the screen. There was a man in a dark business suit, a woman in a red print dress waving at the camera and little Sue Ellen in the blue check dress holding the woman's hand. His hand grabbed the remote and he pressed the volume button.

".... Congressional seat in Ohio's ninth district. The battle will be a tough one for this young republican but the general feeling seems to be that the incumbent has not lived up to his promises and the electorates' expectation. Jim Dewey's announcement of his candidacy is not a surprise. He will have the party's full support in his efforts to get the seat in this perennial democratic strong hold but he has vowed to do it. Back to you, Katie."

The screen filled with Katie Couric's familiar countenance but his words were lost.

She wasn't dead.

She had come back to give him another chance.

He had another opportunity to succeed where he had failed before.

He hurried outside and along the path to the site where he had laid his Sue Ellen to rest years before. He knelt down by the cross he had made and placed his hands upon the leaves that covered her resting place.

"I have another chance. I have another chance. She has come back again."

Tears filled his eyes and dripped down his cheeks into his beard already tinged with gray. He remained there with the tears freely flowing, a sad picture of a desolate man next to two wooden crosses, one large and one small.

Chapter 13

"Dugal, there are some men by the garage. They're wearing waders. They came in a jeep."

It was the first week in May; the perch pond project had been completed for two weeks. Dugal put the paper down, grabbed his coffee cup and went to look out the kitchen window. He stood behind Earleen and could see three men, late twenties or early thirties if he could judge age right, which he couldn't. They were all wearing waders and sweatshirts. Two had baseball caps on and one a stocking cap. They were either smoking or it was cold enough out to see your breath. He knew the latter was true but up here – Up North to most Michiganders – many of the locals still smoked. If you were not a native and had moved here from "civilization" more than likely you didn't smoke – at least on a regular basis. He could see metal cups in at least two hands so there was coffee being drunk but up here who could tell – maybe a wee nip of the hair of the dog to get you going in the morning. Dugal saw the cups being drained and the men starting toward the cabin so he drained his own cup and went out to meet them.

"Morning," he said in greeting his breath turning to smoke as he stepped out the back door. "Can I help you?"

"Morning," retorted the man in the stocking cap. He was at most five foot eight and built like a tank but he was solid. He reached out a hand to Dugal. "John Miller, most people call me Tater…"

"And it's not because he eats a lot of them," one of his companions chipped in.

"Although he does eat a lot of them," the other chimed in.

"Hell, he eats a lot of everything," said the first.

"Would you two hush up," Tater said.

"We're just trying to be neighborly," said the second man.

"… and telling it like it is," retorted the first.

At this juncture, Tater looked to the heavens and said to Dugal, "See what I have to put up with?"

Then he turned to the two and said, "If you want to get paid, keep quiet for a few."

The two looked astonished and then abashed, the first zipped his lips shut and the second clamped both hands over his mouth.

Tater shook his head in apparent despair. "And I have to work with these two."

"And the work is what?" queried Dugal.

"Getting back to that ... I am Tater Miller, hoists and docks are my game. Put them in in the spring and pull them out in the fall."

"Ah," Dugal said. "I was wondering how I was going to do that."

"With us!" Tater exclaimed, waving at his companions. "We used to do it for the Johnsons so I thought you might want us to do it for you. I would have called but you don't have a number that I could find."

"We do but it's a cell phone."

"Ah, so do we have work or should be carry on to our next estate?"

"Well, how much do you charge?"

"Twenty-five dollars apiece. You have a two piece dock or at least the Johnson's did, so that would be fifty dollars."

"In and out?" Dugal asked.

"Nope, fifty in and fifty out."

Dugal thought for a minute.

"I'm going to be getting a pontoon boat ..."

"Almost everyone does," First chimed in.

"... and hoist for ..."

"Your fishing boat under the tarp next to the garage," chimed in Second.

"... my fishing boat," continued Dugal "so they'll have to come out in the fall but we'll deal with that then. I'll make you a deal, Tater. I'll give you eighty bucks now for in and out."

"Cash?" Tater asked.

"Cash," Dugal rejoined.

"Deal," Tater said as they shook hands.

Turning to his companions, he said, "Okay, Derek and my other brother Derek, let's get the day started."

Tater's two companions grinned at each other, "After you, Derek," said Second bowing low with right arm out extending toward the lake.

"No, after you Derek," First said mimicking the bow and then, realizing his mistake, extending his left arm.

"I insist," said Second.

"No ..." stammered First.

At this juncture, Tater hauled off and gave Second a roundhouse kick in this rear and the three headed for the lake, First and Second arm in arm laughing uproariously and Tater trailing behind shaking his head.

Dugal entered the house, grabbing a jacket out of the cloak closet and walking toward the bedroom.

"Who are they?" Earleen asked.

"That's Tater and the Dum Dees," rejoined Dugal.

"Who?"

Dugal stopped to explain.

"Guys who are going to put in and take out the dock and boat hoists. Chuck Shulmann up at Hibbard Marine told me about them when I was in there last week. There are two groups of young men who do this around the lake. Tater and the Dum Dees pretty much take care of the east and south sides of the lake and Rick and the James Gang the west and north."

"But Dum Dees?"

"The two guys John Miller, that's Tater, works with are constantly throwing barbs at whomever is around, each acting as straight man for the other so people refer to them as Tweedle Dum and Tweedle Dee or the Dum Dees."

"They don't look like the Tweedles – more like Mutt and Jeff."

"No, but they act like Tweedles. Anyway Chuck told me about them and suggested that I pay cash in advance in the spring and get a discount. That's what I did. I've been expecting them and have the money all ready."

Dugal headed for the bedroom.

"I'll make another pot of coffee. After being in that cold lake those boys will need it."

Knowing Earleen as he did, Dugal expected this. He got the money and went out the French doors that opened onto the deck. By the time he got to the lake the first section was in and the second was being aligned.

"The Johnsons had their dock right here," Tater said from his managerial spot on the shore. "Is this good for you?"

"I think so, might change it next year but I'll work with it for now."

Tater waded into the lake and helped the Dum Dees fasten the two dock sections together and attached the ramp. The dock was aluminum complete with the decking so it was easy to move into the lake but a slope at the shoreline would make it difficult to move out. The ramp led from the top of the slope to the dock making access easy.

"Quick as a wink..," said Second.

"Time for a drink," chimed in Earleen who appeared beside Dugal with a tray bearing four steaming cups of coffee.

"Wow," said Second, "you're fired" to First "and you, beautiful lady are hired."

The three men clambered out of the lake and up the short hill to grab a steaming mug.

"Anyone need creamer or sugar?" asked Earleen.

"I'm sweet enough but use milk," said First emptying a packet of creamer into his coffee.

"Just as nature make it," said Second sipping carefully at the hot brew. "Man, that's tasty."

"I take both," Tater said. "Learned to drink it as a wee one and had to have both. Used to go hunting with Dad and it was the only thing to warm up. Only had one thermos or I would have taken hot chocolate.

Turning to Dugal, he continued, "Legally I know I wasn't supposed to be with Dad but it was on our own property and I never shot at anything until I was of legal age."

Dugal raised one hand in mock defense.

"Don't worry about me. I don't hunt and I don't work for the DNR so what you did is okay by me."

"But you're a deputy, right?" asked Tater.

"Deputy?" Dugal responded.

"Yeah, when you found the body in the dam at the perch pond the sheriff made you a deputy."

Dugal laughed.

"That? That was just to keep us all in a serious mood."

"But you were there?"

Dugal nodded affirmatively.

"And they say you found the body?"

"Well," Dugal started and then stopped. "Who says?"

Tater looked at the Dum Dees and shrugged. "They … uh, people."

"Well, it was a lucky circumstance. I am not a hero or anything else, just a normal guy who found a skeleton."

"Hey, I understand," Tater said. "Just making conversation and," looking at his watch, "we need to get going. Lots to do today."

"Slam bam," First chimed in putting his mug on the tray.

"Thank you, madam," Second said, following First's lead but taking his hat off and bowing low before her as though royalty.

The Dum Dees then started for the garage.

"Thanks, Tater," Dugal said as he handed the money to Tater. "I guess I call you in the fall when I am ready to have stuff pulled?"

"That'll work," responded Tater handing Dugal a business card and he turned to follow the Dum Dees.

Dugal looked at the card "John's Home Care, Anything you can't do, we can" and a phone number.

"I like them," Earleen said as she headed for the house.

Chapter 14

US-23 splits from I-75 at Ohio Exit 192 north of Bowling Green (home of the Mid-American Conference Bowling Green State University Falcons) and south of Toledo (home of the Mid-American Toledo University Rockets and the AAA baseball Mudhens made famous by the comic character Crankshaft) where for all its four lane divided highway structure and traffic it might as well be an interstate. Its pathway carries northward on the west side of Toledo where it picks up traffic from Exit 59 (formerly Exit 4) of the Ohio Turnpike and then from I-475 which carries traffic between it and I-75 at the point where it turns northeastward toward Michigan and Detroit. Some of the traffic entering US-23 from I-75 has also come from the turnpike via Exit 65 (formerly Exit 4a) onto I-75. US-23 hurries northward through Dundee, Michigan, where Cabalas has build a massive 225,000-square-foot sporting goods store and continues on until just south of Flint where it once again merges with I-75 at Michigan Exit 92. The traffic (which northbound on Fridays and southbound on Sundays during the summer is almost snail paced especially on holiday weekends) then flows northward until US-23 once again splits from I-75 just southwest of Standish at Michigan Exit 188. Then as a two-lane road with occasional passing lanes it turns eastward to the shores of Lake Huron (second largest of the Great Lakes in surface area but third largest in volume) and follows the Michigan coastline northward through Oscoda, Harrisville, east of Hibbard Pond, Alpena, and finally Mackinaw City where it terminates as I-75 crosses the Strait of Mackinac (pronounced Mackinaw) on the five mile long Mackinac Bridge to Michigan's beautiful, isolated, and wild upper peninsula.

About 20 miles north of where it spits from I-75 in Ohio, US-23 passes through the east side of relatively quiet Toledo suburb of Sylvania which lies on the west side of Toledo north of I-475 and northwest of I-75. He had driven his dirty blue

1976 Ford F-150 pickup south to Sylvania following US-23 most of the way.

The trip had taken him two days longer than the ordinary four hours on a typical traffic day because he had been scouting the side roads off most of the exits. He knew that this would be the fastest way to return to the security of his log cabin but he doubted that he would travel on it the entire way. In the recesses of his mind he knew that the law enforcement bodies in Indiana, Michigan, and Ohio would be looking for him – at least they would be looking for someone and he hoped that it wouldn't be him.

His pickup was intentionally dirty and it would be difficult for anyone to identify the color and for most people the make. People nowadays usually identified pickup, SUV, four door, limousine, but didn't get to the technicalities such as Ford, Chevy, Oldsmobile and especially not down to specifics of Ford Ranger, Chevy Caprice, and certainly not down to the year.

He had paid cash for gas and meals (he didn't have a credit card) and slept in the truck pulled way off countryside roads the two nights he had spent on the trip. He was dressed conservatively in new clothes – at least new for him – purchased over the past several weeks in four different second hand stores in four different northern Michigan cities. He didn't like being out of his wooded haven but it was necessary in order to retrieve his little Sue Ellen.

He knew that she couldn't just return to him – this wasn't a miracle birth like that assigned to the Jesus that everyone espoused. He hadn't been raised in a religious environment and what little he knew he had learned in the service and from his own Sue Ellen. He had to retrieve her just as ... he ... had ... before? He thought that but ... he couldn't remember.

He knew that the trip might take several days in Sylvania and several days to get back despite his planning. He had made the trip down to Sylvania twice before, traveling the last part on buses so that his truck wasn't seen and taking different routes down and back each time. He left and returned to his cabin at night so the fewer people that saw him the better it was. Most people – even long time residents and natives – didn't know of his existence anyway. He had no phone and although he had a mailbox at the end of the dirt road, most of his mail was advertising and addressed to "Occupant" or "Resident" except for the occasional notice about his trust.

He had spent almost four days scouting and he knew what his best option was. The first time down he had trimmed his beard to a respectable length and worn new clothes which were burned when he returned to his cabin as he had done after each of his scouting trips. The second time he had a hair cut in Omer (smallest city in Michigan) on the way down. This time his beard was gone and his hair was dyed black.

His Sue Ellen went to day care three days a week – Mom's Helper Day Care. "*Stupid name,*" he thought. Mothers should take care of their kids and not let someone else do it. He had been fortunate on his first trip. Walking past the house he had seen the lady leave with Sue Ellen in the car. Taking the chance that no one was home he had walked to the front door. There was a sticker on the storm door. It showed a fireman carrying a small child away from a house on fire. A label read, "There are ... children in this house." Someone had written in a "1" with a black felt tip marker. At the bottom of the sticker in small print was "Mother's Helper Day Care."

The day care had a playground where the kids played for almost an hour on nice afternoons. There were always two adults with them. When he had been there last week for the second time, the adults were still the same. College co-eds he assumed, maybe teachers-in-training. A brunette and a blonde dressed like college girls in tight fitting skirts (mid-thigh length) and tight tops. At the start of the playtime they were really on top of things. Vigilant to the letter of the word. But after a bit ... Well, they were both smokers and they had to have their smoke. Probably couldn't smoke inside with the kids what with regulations now he knew. They probably weren't supposed to smoke at all but the addiction calls, especially in ones so young. After about 30 minutes (28 the first time and 33 the second) the two aides (couldn't be teachers with that lack of personal discipline he thought) drew to one side secretively and engaged in small talk while cursorily watching the kids and catching up on their habit. This he knew would be his best and only opportunity.

Yesterday he had been in his chosen place, on the side of the play yard opposite where the two had taken their illicit break but one of them had been absent. That side of the play yard had a hedge outside the fence except where there was a gate with a broken lock – he had broken it. Beyond the fence there was a narrow copse of trees and on the other side a small strip mall behind which he had parked his truck. He didn't plan to be there long enough for anyone to notice it and get suspicious. A regular teacher (older and more dedicated) was in the place of the blonde girl and there was no smoke break and no break in vigilance. Today he was hoping for better.

The door to the center opened and the youngsters burst forth onto the playground. There she was, his little Sue Ellen – and he began to feel that maybe today was the day. She was wearing the blue-checked outfit she had been wearing that first day he saw her on TV. Her favorite outfit. She was waiting for him. Almost not breathing he watched the adults come out on the playground. First the brunette who had been there every time, holding the hand of a blonde boy who pulled away and raced for the sand box. The door started to close and then the blonde came out.

He breathed a sigh of relief.

No maybe.

Today *was* the day.

From the shopping bag he had carried with him, he withdrew Reggie, a small brown bear with a pink bow, one eye gone and left leg almost off, the thread having worn away. At least, hers had but this Reggie wasn't hers. He had bought it and carefully made it to look like Reggie, replacing the blue bow with a pink one and aging his Reggie to be her Reggie. After about twenty-five minutes on the playground the two young supervisors had succumbed to habit and drawn off out of sight of the building and lit up.

He was prepared for this and immediately displayed Reggie above the gate and wiggled him. No one noticed. No one except Sue Ellen, just like he had planned. She had caught the movement after about three minutes from where she sat on the edge of the sand box. She had ignored it at first but then had started watching it. After an eternity, it seemed to him, she had started toward the gate, hesitantly at first as though expecting some kind of admonition from her handlers. But there was none and so she continued. Furtively at first and then at an all out run.

By the time she reached the gate, it was open and Reggie was on the ground on the other side. She ran to the bear, not noticing him closing the gate and approaching her from behind, cloth solvent laden ready. He picked her up with his arm around her waist and before she could scream, the cloth was over her face. She kicked, silently screamed. Then she stilled and Reggie dropped to the ground. He stooped, picked up Reggie in the hand with the cloth and headed for the car.

At the edge of the woods, he stopped, picked up the blanket he had put there, shook it out. Laying it on the ground he laid her on it and wrapped her up. Scanning the surroundings he saw no one, nothing out of order, and quickly carried her to the truck and laid her on the passenger side. He closed the door quietly and strode around to the driver's side. He was in and the truck started and he pulled away several minutes before the first alarm sounded at Mom's Helper Day Care.

The police had the place surrounded within fifteen minutes, had discovered the gate with the broken lock in twenty, had followed his trail to the parking lot in thirty and were questioning storeowners and customers. No one had seen anything to do with the case. AMBER Alerts were sounded within twenty minutes but by that time he was in Michigan and on the side roads headed north. He never saw a law official on his entire twelve-hour trip back to the woods. He didn't stop except to fill the tank with gas from five-gallon plastic containers he had purchased at various places during the preceding two weeks. He had packed food to eat as well as water and coffee and he urinated into empty water bottles. The girl slept the entire time, for which he was happy, and didn't wake until the next morning and, of course, there was hell to pay then.

Back in Sylvania the police had nothing to go on. The two teaching aides, both second-year education majors at The University of Toledo, could offer no explanation as to what had happened. They were questioned by both the police and owners of Mom's Helper Day Care and, in the end, were terminated by the day care. Pleas were made by the distraught parents and these, as well as all of the details of the abduction, were carried on national news programs heavily for the first two weeks then semi-weekly for about a month and then sporadically. He knew all this from television that he watched specifically. After the first two weeks, he was confident that he would not be found and turned his full attention to Sue Ellen who had finally realized that she was home and had accepted it.

Chapter 15

Shocking news this morning from Sylvania, OH, a suburb of Toledo. Lynn Dewey, three-year-old daughter of Ohio state Congressman Jim Dewey, currently a candidate for U.S. Representative from the Ohio ninth congressional district, disappeared this afternoon from the playground of Mom's Helper Day Care. Toledo police placed an AMBER Alert for the little girl but as of tonight, just some four hours later, there has been no word.

For those of you not familiar with the AMBER Alert program, it is a voluntary partnership between law-enforcement agencies, broadcasters, and transportation agencies to activate an urgent bulletin in the most serious child-abduction cases. Television and radio use the Emergency Alert System (EAS) to air a description of the abducted child and suspected abductor. The goal of an AMBER Alert is to instantly galvanize the entire community to assist in the search for and safe recovery of the child. This is important because in seventy-six percent of child-abduction homicides, the murder of the child occurs within the first three hours.

The AMBER Alert program has been responsible for 523 successful recoveries. The program consists of 120 plans nationwide of which twenty-three are statewide plans, twenty-nine are regional plans, and thirty-eight are local plans.

Dugal pressed the pause button on his DVR. They were sitting in their great room watching the evening news and eating dinner off TV trays. They had started this practice when they moved into their new home, as the positioning of the television did not permit them to watch as they ate dinner at their table. They had long eaten dinner watching the news in their previous home.

"I was part of the AMBER Alert program the last two years I worked," he said to Earleen. "In 2007, the AMBER Alert Highway Network started distributing these alerts directly to truckers using global-positioning technology. There are thirty-one wireless carriers involved and they cover more than 98 percent of the country."

"Did you ever get one?" Earleen asked.

"Several, as I recall. I'd like to say I helped save a child but never saw any of the suspect vehicles. In this case, according to an earlier report, they didn't have any vehicle description and were just spreading word about the child."

Dugal pressed the pause button to restart the news program.

> *The AMBER Alert program is named for 9-year-old Amber Hagerman who was abducted from her home in Arlington, Texas on January 13, 1996. She was riding her bicycle when a neighbor heard her scream. A man threw her into the front seat of his pickup truck after pulling Amber off her bike, and drove away at a high rate of speed. The police were provided a description of the suspect and his vehicle. Both Arlington police and the FBI interviewed other neighbors, searched for the suspect and vehicle, and local radio and television stations reported the abduction in regular newscasts. Sadly Amber's body was found in a drainage ditch four days later and only four miles away. The kidnapper and murderer have never been found.*

"That's awful," Earleen said.

> *The police chief in Sylvania has asked for help from Team Adam, a program of specially trained retired law-enforcement officers. These officers provide investigative and technical assistance at no cost to law-enforcement agencies or*

assistance given to the victim's family with family advocacy and other personal assistance.

The Team Adam program was named for Adam Walsh, a six year old who went missing and was found murdered in 1981. At this point in time, Team Adam has been deployed 340 times in 45 different states and was extremely helpful in reuniting families split apart by Hurricane Katrina. Adam was the son of Revé and John Walsh, cofounders of the National Center for Missing and Exploited Children. The organization's website is www.missingchildren.com.

In other news, ...

"That sounds like an interesting site," Dugal said. "I wonder if it can be any help in the perch pond case."

Chapter 16

The small fish moved easily through the water, darting side to side as it varied its depth slightly from one and a half to two feet. Occasionally it flicked to the surface as though in search of food. A flash of silver from below and then it was in the mouth of its natural predator – a smallmouth bass.

The smallmouth bass had been cruising the area near a small weed bed in a rocky bottom in search of a meal and had spotted it swimming above its head. A quick flip of its tail and the small fish was dinner. The bass's jump propelled the bass above the water and as it reentered the lake it realized its mistake as the small fish had sunk its treble hook into the bass's mouth.

Dugal's first clue that he had a fish on was the splash about one hundred feet behind him. He immediately swung the tiller of the trolling motor so that the boat turned out toward the middle of the lake and the fish was on the same side as the rod. As part of the same motion he turned the handle to the off position and jerked the rod upward with the other hand. He felt the tension on the line and knew that the Rapala had done its job. Satisfied that the fish was securely hooked, he began to reel it in. It was his fourth bass of the morning of his first day of fishing Hibbard Pond. His hoists had been delivered two days ago and yesterday he and Earleen had put in his boat. They had driven to the DNR boat launch site near the spot where Loon Creek entered Hibbard Pond.

There were about eight empty boat trailers already parked attached to either a pickup truck or SUV but no one was using either of the two docks.

Dugal stopped in the preparation area and got out and readied his boat for launching. Ascertaining that all was well and that the plug was in, he was about to get back in Columbus when he heard, "Morning, sir."

The Body in the Perch Pond

Turning around he saw a DNR officer striding toward him, clipboard in hand. "Making a safety check before you head out this morning."

"No problem," Dugal responded. "What do I need to show you?"

"Let's start with your registration."

Dugal went around the boat to the starboard side, reached into the boat and opened the glove box. He pulled a plastic zip lock bag out, removed the registration and gave it to the officer who had followed him.

"Ohio registration, expires at the end of this year," the officer acknowledged.

"Yes, I bought this near Sandusky in March. I have sent in the registration to the Michigan Secretary of State but haven't received it back yet."

"No problem, the Ohio registration is still good. Let me see a throwable device and one life jacket."

"Sure thing," replied Dugal accommodatingly, and went to the other side of the boat opening a compartment and pulling out a life jacket and an orange plastic object that looked like a Frisbee. "I usually wear a type III device, got one on the driver's seat but you wouldn't count that unless I was wearing it."

"Quite right, sir," replied the DNR officer. "That Personal Retriever throwable is only good if you know how to use it. Want to show me?"

Dugal loosened the line wrapped around the throwable, held it in his left hand and gave the throwable a toss. It sailed thirty feet across the parking lot before hitting the pavement.

"Great, thank you, sir," and Dugal headed for the throwable. "Just one more thing. Can I see your fishing license?"

Dugal reached the throwable, picked it up and started rewinding the cord as he walked back to the boat.

"Sure, let me put this away."

After stowing the throwable, Dugal removed his wallet from his pocket opened it and pulled out his fishing license.

"First one of these I've seen this year," the DNR officer said.

"I buy online and print them every year and laminate them with packaging tape. Save myself something like fifteen percent."

"Thank you, sir," said the DNR officer. "Have a nice day and taut lines."

Dugal got in Columbus and Earleen asked," What was that all about?"

"Just the usual DNR check to be certain I am obeying the law."

He backed the SUV and trailer down and into the water. When the trailer's wheels were in the water, he stopped, Earleen got out and took the rope that Dugal had coiled and left on the boat's bow.

"Ready, Dugal," Earleen called and Dugal backed up until the boat floated free. Then Earleen had walked the line to the middle of the dock and Dugal had pulled forward, the boat sliding easily off the trailer held in place by the rope. Dugal pulled forward until the trailer was out of the water. He got into the fishing boat, lowered the motor that had been tilted to prevent accidently hitting the pavement, and started the engine. The one hundred fifty-horse Mercury roared into life. After letting the motor idle for a minute, Earleen had tossed Dugal the rope and headed for Columbus.

Dugal backed the boat out of the docking area and turned to face the south end of the lake. He was ready to push the throttle and race down the lake when he heard Earleen calling to him. She was standing on the end of the dock waving her arms. He pushed the throttle forward and steered the boat to the end of the dock.

"What's the problem?" he asked.

"Two things, now that you're here. First, I need the keys for Columbus."

"Oops," Dugal said meekly reaching into his pants pocket and handing her the keys. "Habit."

"Thanks, and second, you need to put on your lifejacket."

Dugal grimaced and reached down and picked up the inflatable vest, which he put on.

"Ta ta," Earleen said blowing him a kiss.

He had felt like an idiot for not giving her the keys or putting on the life preserver. The latter contained a small metal *carbon dioxide cartridge designed to get punctured and inflate the vest when it came in contact with water. He had bought two of them and had sworn to wear one when out fishing by himself in case he fell in.*

"Don't want to have to drag the lake for you," Earleen had said when extracting the promise.

Dugal landed the bass without a problem and was happy to see it was a fat sixteen inch one. A keeper in season but that didn't start until Memorial Day still several weeks away. Satisfied with a good two hours of trolling, he decided to go to Hibbard Pond Outfitters and thank Ed for the fishing tips. He turned off the trolling motor, started up the big one and headed for Ed's. He tied up at the dock and walked to the building and opened the back door. He was greeted with a wave of warmth as Ed still had the potbelly going on these cool May mornings.

The place was empty except for Ed behind the counter and Jerry Hatchet leaning on the counter.

"Who did you say again?" Ed said to Jerry.

"A Texan, a Canadian, and a Michigander are out riding horses. The Texan pulls out an expensive bottle of whiskey, takes a drink, then another, and suddenly throws the bottle in the air, pulls out his gun and shoots the bottle in mid air.

"The Canadian looks at him and says, 'What are you doing? That was a perfectly good bottle of whiskey!'

"The Texan says, 'In Texas, there's plenty of whiskey and bottles are cheap.'

"A while later, not wanting to be outdone, the Canadian pulls out a bottle of champagne, takes a few sips, throws the bottle in the air, pulls out his gun and shoots it.

"The Michigander can't believe this and says, 'What did you do that for? That was an expensive bottle of champagne!'

"The Canadian says, 'In Canada there's plenty of champagne and bottles are cheap.'

"So a while later the guy from Michigan pulls out a bottle of beer. He opens it, takes a sip, takes another sip, and then chugs the rest. He then puts the bottle back in his saddlebag, pulls out his gun, turns around and shoots the Canadian.

"The Texan, shocked, says, 'Why did you do that!'

"The guy from Michigan says, 'Well, in Michigan, we have plenty of Canadians, but bottles are worth a dime.' "

Ed gave a good-natured laugh and turned to the door that he had heard opening.

"Hey, Dugal, how you doing? Catching anything?"

"Hi, Ed," responded Dugal. "Jerry," he said acknowledging Hatchet. "Did as a matter of fact. "Four smallmouth and a little walleye. Two of the mouths were keepers, the last sixteen inches."

"Great," said Ed. "That early catch and release DNR program has been great for fishing. How big was the walleye?"

"Thirteen inches."

"Maybe in two years you can catch it again," Ed said with a grin. "Enjoy the walleye while the water is cold. Once it warms up, they go deep."

"How deep?" Dugal asked.

"35-40 feet," Jerry chimed in. "They get below the thermocline which is a layer of cold water separating the really cold from the warm. They just sort of hibernate. You get the bait in front of them or just over them and they'll bite."

"How do you do that?" asked Dugal.

"Lots of ways," replied Jerry. "When the time is right I give you some lessons."

"Great," replied Dugal. "I would appreciate that. Just really getting in to this serious fishing."

"Well, gotta run," Jerry said turning toward the door, "Promised Liz I'd hit the honey do list pretty hard today."

"See youse later," Ed waved.

As the door closed behind Jerry, Ed turned to Dugal.

"What do youse hear about the girl from the perch pond?"

"Why would I hear anything? You're the hub of the lake gossip."

"Me," Ed replied in mock astonishment. "Why women hardly ever come in here."

"Well, their husbands or lovers or both do and guys will talk as much as women if the information is juicy and the girl is a hot topic."

"Yeah, well, information is stagnant and you have a source close to the action."

"Earleen? She doesn't know anything."

Ed chuckled.

"Like hell, but she's not the one I am talking about."

"Then who?"

"The sheriff, your buddy from high school."

"How did …"

"Nevers youse mind. I do and that's a fact."

"Well, that is true but I haven't heard anything for a while."

"Keep in mind that I want to know if you hear anything."

"You'll have to wait your turn," Dugal said laughing. "Got to run, too. My list is probably longer than Jerry's since I just moved in."

Dugal waved as he headed out the door toward his boat.

Chapter 17

"This is an interesting case," Dugal explained to Earleen. He had been looking at the website of the National Center for Missing and Exploited Children for several hours and had noted a couple of the cases to show her.

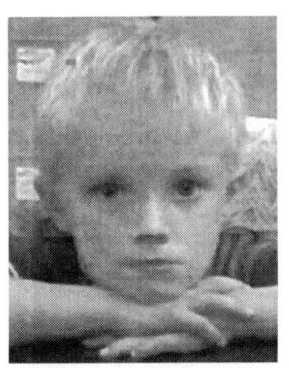

TRISTEN ALLEN MYERS

Age progression
Case Type: Non-Family Abduction
DOB: Jul 16, 1996   **Sex:** Male
Missing Date: Oct 5, 2000   **Race:** White
Age Now: 14   **Height:** 3'1" (94 cm)
Missing City: ROSEBORO   **Weight:** 38 lbs. (17 kg)

Missing State: NC **Hair Color:** Blonde
Missing Country: United States **Eye Color:** Blue
Case Number: NCMC897039
Circumstances: Tristen's photo is shown age-progressed to 11 years. He was last seen walking near his home and may have been walking with a tan Chihuahua and a black Doberman. The dogs were subsequently located. At the time of his disappearance, Tristen was wearing a black T-shirt, blue jeans, and white tennis shoes. He has a scar on the left side of his neck. His full name is Tristen Alan Myers but he uses the nickname "Buddy". He may be in need of medical attention.

"As you can see, Tristen went missing in 2000 and still hasn't been found. What I wanted you to see was the age progression picture. Of course we don't know how accurate it really is but I would think it is reasonably so."

"You know, it looks like something they might do on *Bones*. I always thought it was just to make the show interesting. Have they always been able to do this?" Earleen asked.

"Since 1989 which is only five years after the Center was officially opened by President Reagan."

"This is a non-family abduction, I don't think it bodes well for him being found," Earleen said sadly.

"Interestingly enough," Dugal responded, "In 2008 there were seven long term missing children identified with this technology."

"Wow," Earleen said. "And without it they may have stayed missing."

Dugal continued, "Moreover, NCMEC has a success rate of over 94% while in the mid-90s it was just 62%. Now look at this one, a success story."

Child Located After Three-Year Investigation
A detective with the Central Point Police Department in Central Point, OR contacted the National Center for Missing & Exploited Children (NCMEC) on February 1, 2005 to report that a 17-year-old girl had run away from her foster home. After law enforcement obtained the proper documentation and a photograph of the child, a poster was created featuring the child. The poster was posted on NCMEC's website at www.missingkids.com and distributed in the areas where law enforcement believed the child may travel.

NCMEC continued to work with law enforcement over the next three years to distribute posters, run public database searches, and disseminate information received about the child. A breakthrough in the case came on December 12, 2007, when law enforcement learned the child may have been arrested, but provided an alias name at the time of her arrest. Using both the descriptive information of the child and the arrest photo, law enforcement went to NCMEC's website and compared the information to NCMEC's poster of the child. The photo of the child was then forwarded to the searching mother, who confirmed that it was in fact the missing child. The child was recovered on February 27, 2008.

"I guess that is one of those seven long term cases," Earleen mused.

"I think so," Dugal agreed. "This organization is something else. Did I tell you that the child of one of the cofounders was abducted and found dead?"

"I remember that from the news. His name was Adam."

"Yes," Dugal said. "This is also the organization that made the facial reconstruction of Miss Perch."

"Don't say that, it makes her sound like a beauty queen."

"Sorry, didn't mean to sound so disrespectful but saying 'the girl from the perch pond' or 'Jane Doe' is so impersonal."

"Have they made any progress?"

"Not that I know of. A representative of Team Adam was around here during the first couple of weeks but as far as I know, there is nothing else.

Chapter 18

"May we join you?" Dugal looked up and saw a pretty black lady in a flowery yellow print dress standing next to their table. She wasn't petit but she wasn't a size 14 either and behind her, impossible to hide because of his size, stood Nathanial, nattily dressed in blue blazer, tan slacks, and yellow shirt open at the neck.

Dugal stood up and offered her the chair next to him.

"Certainly. You must be Dawn. I'm Dugal McBruce and this is my wife Earleen."

Dawn sat down and Nathanial moved around the table and took the seat opposite her.

"Nathanial has said so much about you, I am glad I had this chance to meet you."

It was Mother's Day and Dugal had taken Earleen to the brunch at the Loon Creek Inn. It was a beautiful day and they were seated at a table by the window, Dugal having made reservations in early April. The inn was situated lakeside and had a broad veranda – its tables having umbrellas for sunny weather. From the veranda a series of wooden steps and landings led to the lake where a dock with room for ten boats was empty today but would be full on weekend evenings as the weekenders would take advantage of the weather to be on the lake every possible minute. In 1843 Captain Mills Baker, retired from the military and wanted an isolated place to live away from the crowded cities with their constantly bickering populace, built a log cabin on the site of what is now the Loon Creek Inn. It burned to the ground in 1855 and the basic structure of the current building was put in its place as the area was beginning to be populated. Initially known as Baker's Tavern, its name was changed to Hibbard Pond Inn in the early 1900s when Baker's son sold it. That name stayed until the 1970s when new owners added to it and, enamored with the birds that used the creek as a nesting ground, named it for them. The Loon Creek DNR launch site from which Dugal had launched his fishing boat Taut Lines was almost directly eastward across the lake and to the left (north) was the mouth of Loon Creek. Signs everywhere warned boaters this was a no wake zone because of the loons who bred up creek and within 100 feet of the mouth there was a string of buoys to keep boats away during the breeding season. By the end of the summer the buoys would be removed and the creek would be available to fishermen and duck hunters.

"We're so glad you wanted to join us," Earleen said. "I have been meaning to call to offer my help in Nathanial's campaign."

"We're really just getting started in that. I ordered the campaign yard signs on Friday." She smiled at Nathanial. "He is really nervous about this. He's never run for elected office before."

"That's not quite true," Dugal said. "He was elected homecoming king our senior year."

Nathanial said nothing.

"Oh, that," Dawn quipped in a pooh poohing manner. "That's was just a popularity contest."

"And what's this," asked Dugal good naturedly pointing at Nathanial. "He has to be the most popular sheriff in the county!"

Nathanial glared sarcastically at Dugal.

"This is serious, Dugal," Earleen said. "Quit the boyish stuff and be serious."

And to Dawn.

"What party is Nathanial running with, not that it matters one whit to us."

"I am not affiliated with any party," interjected Nathanial. Then to Dugal "And it is serious."

"I know," Dugal said.

"I am running as an independent," continued Nathanial. "Historically this is a strongly Republican county except in the sheriff's election. Then it tends to be anything but. My opponent is a Republican, or at least when he runs for sheriff but, as you can see, it hasn't helped. My predecessor was an independent and that's my choice. I am not political at all, can't stand politics and don't want to be – won't be – beholding to anyone after the election."

"So," Dugal responded. "Do you have a platform? Any planks?"

"Just to run an efficient and honest sheriff's department. There is enough corruption in politics, even in this backward – oops, make that low income – county. The department is there to enforce the laws and protect the citizens and their property."

"You sound as though there is trouble brewing," Earleen said and looked at Dawn who had a positively radiant but unrevealing poker face.

"Nothing that I can talk about at this time."

"Are you folks ready to order? My name is Janet and I'll be taking care of you today."

Opportunely the waitress had come to the table.

"We would like," Dugal said, indicating himself and Earleen as though there was any doubt, "a V8-juice for her, orange juice and coffee for me. We'll both have the buffet."

"We don't have V8," Janet said. "We have tomato or Bloody Mary Mix."

Earleen made a face. "I'll have the tomato then."

"And you, Mrs. Jefferson," Janet said to Dawn.

Dawn looked surprised but only momentarily, "Orange juice and hot tea with lemon."

"Sheriff?"

"Coffee, no cream or sugar. And we'll have the buffet. Been hearing good things about it."

"Fine. You can all go to the buffet, no one is there now and I'll have your drinks on the table before you get back."

As the couples stood up, Earleen said to Dawn, "Well, obviously if you're the wife of the sheriff, you are known to all."

"That," replied Dawn, with an impish smile, "Or it's my tan."

The offerings were scrumptious and bountiful with pancakes, Belgian waffles, blueberry muffins, popovers, croissants, scrambled eggs, omelets made to order by a young man who didn't appear to be old enough to shave, bacon both regular and Canadian, five different fruits, baked whitefish, beef bourguignon, lasagna both meat and vegetarian, four different vegetables, prime rib cut as you wanted it, and on a separate table six different deserts including chocolate mousse and strawberry cheese cake.

"I think I've died and gone to heaven," Nathanial said putting down a plate over laden with food, "and I only took half of what I wanted."

Dugal, who had judiciously gone for the prime rib, bacon and scrambled eggs, two popovers and a bowl of fresh strawberries, looked at Nathanial's plate and said, "Don't they pay you enough to put food on the table?"

"He always eats that way at a buffet," Dawn explained putting down a plate with a mushroom and cheese omelet, two slices of Canadian bacon and a bowl of blueberries. "He'll diet for a week to make it possible."

"That's enough food to feed us for a week," Earleen said looking at her plate of scrambled eggs, bacon, blueberry muffin and a bowl of fruit cocktail. "I'm saving room for the cheese cake, my absolute favorite."

"I'm just a growing boy," Nathanial said as he started to dig in.

"But which way?" chided Dugal as he took his first bite of prime rib.

The meal was enjoyed heartily by all with good-natured bantering and conversation continuing as though the four had been lifelong friends. Following the ritual of paying the bill, the four walked casually to their cars.

"Anything new on our young lady," Dugal asked. "I didn't want to talk business in there."

"Appreciate that and no, nothing for publication," replied Nathanial. "However, off the record and just between us, although I know the word will get out, we have no DNA match on file anywhere. If she disappeared about the time of her death there should be a sample from her parents or something but there is nothing."

"Strange," Dugal said. "She could have been adopted"

"True, that is one explanation. The other," Nathanial continued, "is that she had gone missing prior to prevalent DNA or that her parents wouldn't give a sample."

"What parents wouldn't want to do that to help find out what happened to their daughter?" Earleen asked.

"Folks are unusual," answered Nathanial. "I have a feeling that it is going to take something strange to get to the bottom of this one."

"Maybe," Nathanial responded, "but the Cold Case Unit from the Center for Missing and Exploited Children is tackling it. They're a good group. They've helped resolve more than 359 long-term cases since 2001. In fact, one of them was as old as 1947. If anyone can get to the bottom of this case, it's going to be them."

"Yes," Dugal agreed, "I've looked at their website. They have done some fantastic things."

Chapter 19

"Mornin', neighbor. Mighty fine day, eh?"

It was late May, just a couple of days before the Memorial Day weekend and Dugal was in the open area north of the house preparing to rototill a garden for Earleen. He had brought his rototiller down from the garage, started it, and then turned it off while he put his gloves on. He looked up toward the sound of the voice and saw a man approaching from the house to the north.

"Morning," Dugal said. "You must be Herbert Smythe. Irene Stockwell told us about you."

Walking up to Dugal and extending his hand, he replied "Yep, that'll be me."

Dugal removed the glove he had just put on and grasped the proffered hand.

"Dugal McBruce, my wife is Earleen, we moved here in early March. Glad to meet you. Is it Herb or Herbert?"

"Neither," Smythe responded. "Years ago I picked up a nickname from one of your American sitcoms. Can you guess, eh?"

Dugal looked wonderingly at him then ... "Norm! From *Cheers*," Smythe exclaimed. "Yep, that's it and I can't shake it."

"You folks are from Canada, if I recall correctly."

"Yes, over near Toronto, place named Kitchener. Been coming here summers for over fifteen years. Be retiring next year but the habit probably won't change. Folks had the place and we inherited. We like to tell folks that we go south in the winter, eh." He laughed.

"You sound just like him when you laugh," Dugal said.

"Who?" asked Norm.

"Norm from *Cheers*."

"Oh, yeah," Norm said hitting himself in the head. "Not my choice of nicknames but have to live with it."

The Body in the Perch Pond

"You must have gotten in late last night."

"Yep, about 10:00. Got a late start. Then worked until almost midnight getting everything unloaded. I'm an early riser. Pauline is still in bed and probably will be for another hour or so. Luckily I know how to make coffee."

Norm held up a travel cup in his left hand and took a sip. From the lake, a loon called.

"Ah, my first of the year. Love those birds, don't you?"

"Yes, they certainly have strange calls."

"You know the story of how those calls came to be?"

"Can't said that I do ..." and Norm launched into his story.

"The Northwest Indians say that when the world was young, Loon had the most beautiful voice of all the people. They came from all around to hear her sing. But the evil spirits showed up and stole daylight. The world grew cold. Trees lost their leaves. The river froze over and the sky got black dark. Evil spirits kept daylight in a cedar box behind a wall of ice, and things looked dire. Raven, the boss, called a conference of all the people to see what they could do.

"Osprey tried to reach daylight by soaring high above the ice wall, but the evil spirits threw shrill winds at her and she came back shaggy of feather and defeated. That wasn't the way to do it. Deer tried to burst through the ice wall with his antlers, but he returned minus his antlers, head bloodied. That wasn't the way to do it either. Bear, against Raven's advice, challenged the evil spirits to a wrestling match. But the evil spirits cleaned his clock. Bear staggered back, crawled into a cave, and slept.

"Violence, Raven told the people, wasn't the way. They would have to be clever.

"Loon had an idea. Mole, with his sharp claws, could tunnel under the ice wall and make a hole big enough for Loon to slip through. Mole couldn't see far and had to be led by Loon to the spot, but they did it. Loon reached the box that held daylight. She lifted the lid. Daylight escaped, which alerted the evil spirits, who recaptured daylight and then grabbed Loon by the beak and threw her over the wall, stretching her neck.

"Loon's tactic, however, proved sound. Raven herself tunneled beneath the ice wall and opened the cedar box. Sheltering daylight under a broad black wing, she put it back in the world. The world warmed up. The ice wall melted into the river. Seeds stirred in the earth, and the trees began to bud. Daylight was back, and all the people were happy.

"'Sing us your song,' the people said to Loon. 'It's time to celebrate.'

"Loon began to sing, but it was a most horrid and embarrassing sound. Her neck and voice box, stretched, were damaged beyond repair. The people looked away, pretending not to hear. But Loon told them the loss of her voice was a small price to pay for helping bring daylight back to the world. The people soon saw it her way, and Loon became a great hero. Today, whenever darkness nears, Loon remembers the time the evil spirits stole daylight, and you can hear her haunting call across the water.

"That's what those Northwest Indians say, anyway," Norm concluded. "You know, those folks with the totem poles, eh."

"Aleuts," injected Dugal.

"Yep, that's right. Interesting people, been there twice, once on a cruise and once a land tour. You hunt?"

"No, I …"

"I don't either, Pauline's the hunter. Keeps the larder stocked. Hunts with the boys both here and in Canada."

"Boys?" queried Dugal fighting to keep in the conversation.

"Yep, two, big strapping lads. They'll be up this weekend to put the dock and hoist in. I'll have to get the powerboat and Jet Ski ready. Anyway, they and Pauline hunt for deer here and in Canada and bear in Canada. Pauline got a bear last year."

"Really, …"

"Yep, big black bear. Having the skin made into a rug. Have to keep the boys' dogs off it."

"Dogs…"

"Yep, Ben has one and Jonathon two. Ben's married, Jonathon's not," he paused.

Given the chance, Dugal injected, "Well, I really need to get this tilling done. Earleen's got stuff ready to plant and I still need to do a fence."

While Norm was talking, Dugal had put his gloves on. He pushed the throttle lever and choke to full and pulled the cord. The tiller's engine roared to life loudly drowning out Norm's continuing onslaught. Throttling back on the choke, Dugal put the tiller into gear and the tines started churning. Within two steps, he realized he hadn't set the drag stake to slow the tiller down, so he took the tiller out of gear, set the stake, and was off. At the end of the first row, he saw Norm still standing there but was uncertain if he was still talking. He took the tiller out of gear, lifted the handles, pulling the drag stake out of the ground and turned the tiller to the left, reset the stake and put the tiller into gear. At the end of the bottom of the garden, he performed another turn and noticed that Norm was on the way back to his house.

He kept at it until he had tilled the garden three times to be certain that he was deep enough and there were no big clods of earth. Stones of all sizes he had found aplenty from pebbles to softballs. Those were Earleen's problem. Finishing the tilling he walked the tiller to the back of the pump shed, turned on the hose and washed it off. Ten years and he had never had a problem.

Peeling his gloves off, he went to the back door, unlaced his boots and stepped inside. Closing the door behind him, he stepped out of his boots and opened the door to the great room. His senses were tingled by the smell of fresh bread.

"That smells great," he said. "French bread?"

He knew the answer as Earleen had started on it when he went out.

"Almost ready?" he asked hungrily. "Met our neighbor."

"So I saw and heard," Earleen said.

"Heard?"

"Yes, I was coming out to see how it was going and heard him yakking – no other way to describe it – so I turned around."

"Sure hope that Pauline is the silent type."

"Or," mused Earleen, "maybe she is talkative so that he can't get a word in edgewise and makes up for it when she isn't around."

"Then let us be certain that she is always around," Dugal said.

*****

The answer to their concerns came sooner than expected. After a brief rest with a glass of milk and several pieces of piping hot fresh French bread laden with butter and Earleen's strawberry jam, both of them were outside working on the garden. Earleen was planting and Dugal setting posts for the fence he hoped would keep out the deer and small critters. He had gone to the garage with the wheelbarrow for the last of the treated four by fours he was using as the fence posts. As he returned with the last four posts, he noticed Earleen standing in the middle of her garden talking to a young teenage girl. It was only when he got closer that he realized that the girl was a woman and she certainly was not a teenager. He stopped the wheelbarrow by a posthole and released the handles causing the wheelbarrow to settle with a distinctive thump and rattle of posts.

He looked at the two women who hadn't even seemed to notice him. He picked a post up and was getting ready to set it into the hole when Earleen called to him.

"Dugal, come meet Pauline. She has something interesting to tell you."

Dugal complied after setting the pole into the hole and pulling off his gloves as he walked to the middle of the garden, gingerly avoiding the plants that Earleen already had in the ground, and eyeing Pauline who was the physical antithesis of her husband and, he hoped, verbal also.

"Glad to meet you, Dugal," Pauline said. "I know that you already met Herb or Norm as he likes to be called. He probably told you it was a nickname but not that he gave it to himself. He loved *Cheers* and grew attached to Norm. I am the only one who hasn't changed.

"Also when he first meets someone, he feels he has to make a good impression so he tends to overwhelm them with his knowledge. After a time or two that wears off, hopefully, before he estranges his new acquaintance.

"Well, you two are busy and I have a lot to do. See ya, eh!"

She turned with a wave behind her and trotted toward her home.

"She's nice," Earleen said. "She was concerned with the impression that Norm made so she wanted to explain. He has a big mower and bagger and is going dump clippings near the garden when I decide on a spot. I will use them as ground cover to keep weeds away, except for your potatoes, and make a compost heap. Nothing like being green."

With that, she went back to planting and Dugal stood there, the target of verbal battering for the second time that morning. *"There ought to be a law,"* he thought. Then he shrugged and turned back to his fence post.

From behind the Smythes's house he heard a mower roar to life. *"So much for the quiet of the woods,"* he thought.

Chapter 20

"Hard to believe that just a couple of months ago, this was just a farm pond, and now it's a perch hatchery."

Jerry Hatchet and Dugal were in a small rowboat in the middle of the perch pond. Dugal was rowing and Jerry was in the back tossing handfuls of grain onto the surface of the water. Dugal just grunted in response. He wished he had worn gloves as his hands were starting to blister after an hour of rowing.

"Next time, you get to row," Dugal said.

"Hey, that's manual work. I'm retired, don't ask me to do a damn thing that involves that four letter wood."

"Yeah, that is Liz's complaint about you in retirement. Long to do list and no honey to be found."

"Who you been talking to? One of those anti-Jerry-ites?"

"What?"

"The place is teeming with them. Those local …"

"Cut it out, Jerry. Enough of the bull shit. Keep throwing the seed and shut your mouth. When you talk, you stop throwing."

Jerry cast several handfuls of seed while Dugal rowed several strokes.

"I never would have bothered with that piece of plastic," Jerry proffered. "If it had been me, that body wouldn't have been discovered."

Dugal paused his rowing.

"I've thought about that. Don't know what made me look at the plastic. There was just this nudge from inside. Looking back on it, I am glad I did. If I hadn't, she might not have been discovered and then she would still be lying at the bottom of the dam covered with the outlet pipe. Probably for the rest of eternity."

They sat thoughtless for a moment with the ominous weight of that idea upon them.

"I am glad you found her as now maybe she or her spirit can find some peace. That's the good side. On the other side, if you hadn't pull that piece of plastic then this place wouldn't have been discovered."

This last remark was made in reference to the fact that for several weeks after the discovery reporters from two downstate papers and a national paper had been in the area asking about the murder.

"Still hasn't been discovered. You worry too much, Jerry. This place is so hard to get to you have to use a GPS." Dugal took a couple of more stokes.

"Any hope of you finishing ..."

"Look at those turtles," Jerry interrupted.

Dugal looked where Jerry was pointing. They were about four feet from a bank and nearer the shore were two large turtles with shells at least as big as a basketball.

"Huge – snapping turtles, I think," said Dugal. "Look at the evil eye that one is giving us. Looks like he wants to bite our hands off."

"Or something else," Jerry agreed. "It almost looks like that one is mounting the other. Is that how turtles do it?"

"Don't know but let's leave them alone."

A couple of strokes of the oars and the snappers had their privacy.

"So you talked to any reporters?" Jerry asked.

"One came to the house about three days after the discovery when the news was hot," Dugal answered. "Wanted to ask me questions and I told her I didn't know anything. At that point I believe we were still under sheriff's orders to keep quiet or at least that's what I told her. She persisted but I did also and she left."

"What paper?" Jerry asked.

"Free Press," Dugal answered. "Of course that would get to the News and possibly USA Today."

"You could have had your five minutes of fame or maybe in your case, shame."

"What about the other ten?"

"What other ten?" Jerry asked.

"It's fifteen minutes of fame," Dugal answered. "Supposedly in 1968 at an international exhibition in Stockholm, Andy

Warhol said, 'In the future everybody will be world famous for fifteen minutes.' "

"Andy Warhol," mused Jerry facetiously. "Who the hell was he?"

"I don't know. All I know is that he made that statement."

The two looked at each other and then burst out laughing. Dugal went back to rowing and Jerry back to seeding the pond.

Chapter 21

"Fish on," Jerry shouted, "Middle line left."

Dugal leapt up where he had been sitting in one of the fishing chairs on Jerry's pontoon boat and grabbed the middle fishing rod. The line had whipped from its position in the middle of the planar board line and was trailing at the rear of the boat. Dugal looked at the line counter, that read 145 feet and began reeling.

"It's heavy, definitely a fish."

This was the third line that had snapped that morning: the first was one that Dugal had put on incorrectly and was not even fully set before the fishing line pulled loose from the clip on the planar board line; the second was one of Jerry's and it had held a small walleye.

The two had been out on the lake over an hour, the first half of which Jerry had explained the set up of the planar boards and how they were used.

"People have different techniques. Most people use the individual boards, usually yellow or orange plastic with a red flag. Supposedly when a fish hits those, its weight will 1) pull the flag down and/or 2) pull the board toward the back of the boat and thus in.

"I tried and couldn't get it to work for me. The fish I caught didn't lower the flag or pull the board back. I only knew there was a fish on by pulling the darn thing in and that's a lot of work. First you get the board in and you have to remove it and then you still have 100 feet of line or so to pull in. So I went to the type they use on the big lakes. Bought the six-foot pole with two reels of line. Made the planar boards myself.

"The process is simple, you attach the planar boards to the planar board line and let them out about fifty to seventy-five feet. Then you let your line out about 100 feet, put one of the sliding rings on the planar board line, put your line in the clip, and let it out to where you want it to be. When the fish

bites (and you put it on correctly which takes a little practice) the line slips out of the clip and the fish pulls it alongside the boat."

And so they had begun, with Dugal handling the helm while Jerry rigged up his lines, showing Dugal each step. Dugal had taken twice as long as Jerry and had inadvertently dropped one of the clips into the water.

"Hey, matey," Jerry had said with the ring of a true salt in his voice, "that's coming out of your pay. Drops another and we'll keel haul ye."

Dugal wound the reel and finally saw the fish break the surface about twenty feet in back of the boat.

"Looks like a keeper, Dugal," Jerry shouted. When the fish was about five feet from the stern, Jerry got up and went to the back through the gate, took the long handled net out of its holder, and with seemingly practiced ease, netted the walleye as Dugal brought it parallel with the stern.

"Definitely a keeper," Jerry shouted eagerly as he moved the net to where Dugal could retrieve the fish.

"He spit out the hook," Dugal said. "Glad you were so handy with the net." Securing the walleye with fingers through its gills, Dugal lifted it out of the net and laid it on the yardstick that Jerry had screwed to the deck.

"Seventeen and a quarter inches. Keeper."

Dugal opened the lid of the live well, and put the fish in. Wiping his hands on his trousers like any good fisherman, he high-fived with Jerry and set about getting the line reset. When it was done, he resumed his seat.

"That was fun. Let's do it again."

"Hope to do it many more times today," Jerry said.

"You'll have to teach me to filet it properly."

"That's a snap," Jerry said. "You could probably pick it up off a U-tube video but I'll show you a better way, guaranteed."

It was a beautiful mid-July day, partly cloudy with just a slight breeze to make six-inch waves. Only two other boats were to be seen.

"It's interesting," Dugal noted, "that during the week, there are few fishermen but come the weekend the lake is loaded with boats and PWCs."

"Yep, this is weekend heaven for downstaters. Be glad that every weekend is not like Memorial Day or Fourth of July weekend. I don't go out any weekend. I use the weekdays for my pleasure and let the downstaters rule the lake on the weekends."

"My thoughts exactly," Dugal replied.

Both men were silent for a while.

"You know, I've been thinking a lot about that young lady from the perch pond. I figure that she was abducted or ran away. Definitely not from around here or somebody would have said something."

"Unless that somebody was the somebody who put the body under the dam."

"Yes, true, but don't you think that at that age she would have friends, family, be missed."

"Maybe she was home schooled."

"Well, could be. I found this site on the web missingkids.com, the website of The National Center for Missing & Exploited Children. Did you ever hear of it?"

"No, I don't have internet access."

"But you said you downloaded the planar board plans from the web."

"True, but I went to the library in Lincoln to do it."

"Got you," Dugal said. "Anyway I was doing some looking and got some startling facts. Let's see. They say that 1 of every 5 girls and 1 of every 10 boys will be sexually victimized before they are 18."

"That's a lot," Jerry said.

"The startling fact is that only 1 in 3 will report it."

Jerry was quiet, a distant and disquieting look on his face.

"What's wrong, Jerry?" Dugal said.

For a moment Jerry did not respond.

"It's not easy to tell someone if someone has made advances toward you," he said. "It's hard. Like telling your mother you have something wrong with your penis cause then you know you'll have to show her."

Dugal looked at him.

"You were sexually abused?"

Jerry was silent. He was struggling with something, Dugal could tell. Jerry took a deep breath.

"I haven't known you very long but I think we're good friends."

"Yes, we are," Dugal agreed.

"You have to promise not to tell anyone. Well, anyone except your wife. If you're at all like me and Liz, you don't – hell, you can't – keep secrets."

"Yeah, we'd be talking about something related and I would show something on my face and she wouldn't let up until I tell her. She is the same way. Been married too long I guess."

"Maybe but I think that is a good thing. If you had a secret you couldn't tell her, it would eat you up inside. It certainly does me."

"Well, if you don't feel like telling me don't. I understand; it's personal."

"No, I need to tell now that I have gone this far. It really isn't that bad. My fifth grade teacher was Mr. Swartz, Jim Swartz. He was young, only been teaching a couple of years. I really liked him. One day he asked me to stay after school to get help with my mathematics. I wasn't too good then and – truthfully – aren't much better now. If I add 2 and 3 and get 6 two days running, that's a record."

"But ..." Dugal chimed in.

"I know. 2 plus 3 is 5, at least today. It's just that numbers and I don't communicate but that's not important. We worked for a while and then he said he had to go to the bathroom and said that since no one was here, I had to go with him. I had to go, too, and thought it would be neat because we were going to the teachers' bathroom. Of course there were two; men and women. There were three urinals and he took the middle one. I held back but he told me not to be shy. So I unzipped, peed and put it back. Trying not to look but I got a look at his and my mouth must have dropped. You know that to a fifth grader, an adult's looks big. He saw me looking, he'd been waiting for me to; I know now. In fact, I don't think he peed at all. He smiled at me, 'You'll have one this big when you grow up. Want to touch it?'

"I thought about it just for a flick of a second, then I caught the look on his face. I didn't know how to describe it, lascivious I guess now that I know the word. Whatever it was, I knew it wasn't nice and I bolted. I think the only reason I got out that door was that he put his back in first. I ran down the hall, threw my weight against the bar on the front door and burst out of the building.

"I ran and ran and ran, all the way home. That was a long way, I usually took a bus. I didn't say anything to mom or dad but they thought something was wrong. Next morning I complained about a stomachache and my mother believed me or thought that I was troubled enough to stay home. It took a lot of coaxing and talking to get me to tell her. And then all hell broke loose – she called the principal but only after she called dad. They called the superintendent; they called the police. I had to talk to them and tell them what happened. You think that's easy? I'll tell you it wasn't."

Dugal shook his head as though struggling with the story. "I know it wasn't. I don't know what I would have done."

Jerry laughed, "Looking back on it I know I should have touched the thing."

"What!" Dugal exclaimed.

"I should have touched it and then hit him in the balls. That's what I would have done if I knew what I know now, but I didn't."

"Well, what happened?"

"Mr. Swartz didn't come back to school after that. We had a permanent substitute. An old biddy named Mrs. Smythe, Mrs. Thelma Smythe.

"My neighbor's name is Smythe," Dugal said. "Was she Canadian?"

"She was a Brit, from Liverpool, and really a nice lady I know now but we gave her a devil of a time."

"What about the teacher?"

"Nobody ever told me – just that he wasn't teaching any more. I have never bothered trying to find out. I try not to think about it very much."

"Did you ever tell your friends?"

"Nope not a … fish on, my side. Take the helm, Dugal."

Chapter 22

"So is this the famous perch pond?"

The weather thus far in August had been unseasonably cool necessitating sweatshirts when outside and even heavier jackets out on the lake. The past few days had been milder with clear skies and bright sun. Earleen had suggested that their weekly bike tour be to the perch pond, as she had never seen it. A fairly easy ride of thirty minutes had brought them to the dam.

"Yes," Dugal said. "This is it."

"Where was the skeleton found?"

"Follow me."

Taking her hand, he led her down the slight slope of the backside of the dam dotted with patches of mud and grass, stopping near the top of the access tube to the guillotine gate.

"Basically the skeleton lay at the bottom of this tube," Dugal explained. "Tim was starting to clear out the area when the backhoe's scoop brought up the head."

Earleen eased her way to look at the access tube, the top of which was covered by a metal grate welded together from reinforcing rod and fastened to the pipe with chains and padlocks.

"Is it the handiwork of George Jameson?"

"Yes, he is quite the fabricator. Don't know how we would have done some of this without him."

"Oh, I can see some perch," Earleen squealed looking into the water near the gate where a school of small fish could be seen.

"Or minnows," Dugal said. "I can't be certain."

"Right, Mr. Always Correct, spoiling the fun. Hold my hand, I want to get down closer to the water for a better look."

Tall grasses were growing along the slight inlet made by the access pipe and the grassy areas were slick from the morning's dew. Dugal offered his hand and they eased their way down the slope.

Suddenly Earleen jumped back with a squeal, knocking Dugal to the ground and falling on top of him.

"What's this all about?" Dugal said. "This is neither the time nor the place."

"Don't be a ninny," Earleen said. "It's just turtles."

They got up, brushing dew and mud from their clothes and Dugal looked down into the inlet. He found himself looking at a couple of huge turtles, one of which was glaring at him malevolently.

"They look like the same pair that Jerry and I saw when we were spreading feed. Of course with a pond this big there are probably more than just two."

"They look mean," Earleen said, beginning to try to get back up the slope.

Dugal took her hand and together they carefully climbed the slight but slippery slope.

"I wouldn't want to slip and slide into that ... Oh..." she gasped.

"What now?" Dugal asked as he followed her gaze and immediately saw what she had seen.

Earleen was looking at a huge deer that was standing about halfway to a line of trees about a hundred yards away.

"That thing is huge," Earleen breathed. "I've never seen such a huge stag."

"It has an immense spread," Dugal said. "He's been around for a while."

The two then stood in silence watching the stag watching them for several minutes. Then slowly it turned and walked toward the woods. Every ten feet or so it would pause briefly and look back. Finally as it reached the tree line, it stopped and looked back at them for a minute. Then he shook his head as though in agreement and majestically disappeared into the woods.

"He almost acted like he wanted us to follow him," Earleen mused. "You know, stopping and looking back and then finally that shake of his head. It could be a nod but maybe a 'let's go'!"

When Dugal didn't answer she turned to look at him and found him staring at the ground where there were definitely king sized deer hoof prints.

"He was here," Earleen said.

"Yes," answered Dugal. "But that doesn't mean anything. There is grass and water here."

He paused, musing.

"Still…"

*****

A few days later during one of their biweekly fishing expeditions, Dugal mentioned the episode to Jerry.

"Hmmm," mused Jerry. "That sounds like about where I thought I saw the man when we were recovering the bones."

"You thought you saw?"

"Well, I was never certain. I looked up and caught movement in that direction and looked. I thought I saw someone step back into the woods. It could have been a deer but with all the activity, the noise of the backhoe and all, I wouldn't have thought so."

"Did you tell the sheriff?" Dugal asked.

"He asked me about it and I told him. He said he would check it out. He went back there but didn't find anything other than a possible animal path but they're all over the place. He said if I couldn't be more descriptive, it wasn't anything he could follow up … Fish on, my side. Take the con, Dugal."

Chapter 23

The meeting room in the Lincoln Senior Citizens Center was abuzz as the assembled crowd waited for the highlight of the League of Women Voters Candidates' Podium Night 2010, the candidates for Sheriff of Alcona County. Already the candidates for road commissioner, county trustees, and various township offices had taken the podium, made their presentations, and answered questions limited to five minutes per office, not per candidate because of the number of offices. Standing room only tonight, an unusual occurrence as most elections were humdrum and getting voters to the polls quite difficult. However this election seemed different. It was mid-August, almost four months since the discovery of the body in the perch pond but there had been no progress made in finding her identity or her killer. Everyone knew this. In fact, just in the prior week there had been an editorial in the Alcona Review on the subject and an op-ed piece in the Alpena News. These certainly were adding fuel to the fire.

Dugal and Earleen were seated about halfway back from the stage, intentionally distancing themselves from Dawn who sat in the first row with other spouses of candidates. Behind Dawn sat their son and his family, safely home from Afghanistan he had taken this opportunity to visit his parents. Although some of the crowd in the room knew of the relationship between Dugal and Nathanial, most of them didn't. Dugal had a job that night – anything that Leonard Hilbreth said that at all questioned Nathanial's integrity or work on the job was supposed to be questioned during the five minute period allotted for that. At least if Dugal knew that Nathanial could effectively retort.

The buzz hushed as the evening's hostess Ellen McGinty, President of the local chapter of the League of Women Voters, stepped to the podium.

"Our final candidates of the evening are Nathanial Jefferson and Leonard Hilbreth, candidates for sheriff. Prior to this evening's proceedings, as with all the candidates for office if there was a contest, a coin flip determined the first speaker."

She turned to Nathanial, "Mr. Jefferson."

Nathanial stepped to the podium, resplendent in his uniform. He looked at the audience, his eyes scanning it completely and finally settled on his son first and then his wife Dawn. He smiled at her and began.

"Thank you, madam chairperson, it was a pleasure to be invited here tonight. My name is Nathanial Jefferson. As all of you know, I am currently acting sheriff of Alcona County because the heart attack suffered by Sheriff Collins a year ago this past spring incapacitated him and forced him to retire. I have been a member of the sheriff's department for eleven years. I grew up in suburban Detroit, attended State for one semester and then joined the highway patrol. Someone is bound to ask why I left State and it is quite simple. I had a football scholarship and suffered a career-ending injury in my first semester. Rehabilitation took over eight months and, although my tuition would have been paid, my family and I did not have the resources for me to continue. Regardless I was headed for a law enforcement career ..." here he chuckled softly " ... unless I had been fortunate enough to try for a career in the NFL.

"After serving twenty years with the patrol, I took retirement and applied for an opening here and was accepted. My wife Dawn and I have established our home here, living in Greenbush.

"Probably everyone wants to know what I will do if I am elected. It is simple – I will continue to run the office in an efficient and effective manner, providing security and protecting the safety of all residents and visitors to our county. I have no changes to make. Our force is well trained and effective in their jobs. We are currently one person short. If I am elected, I will find a qualified individual to fill that position, and if my opponent is elected, he will fill the sheriff's position and I will go back to being a deputy.

"Thank you for your consideration."

He nodded to Leonard Hilbreth and Ellen McGinty, and resumed his seat to modest applause from the audience. He smiled at Dawn and his son and Dugal thought he perceived a slight shrug of his shoulders but possibly that was just him settling in. Ellen McGinty came to the podium again.

She turned to Leonard Hilbreth, "Mr. Hilbreth."

Leonard Hilbreth pushed himself to his feet and brusquely strode the few steps to the podium.

"Ellen, Mr. Jefferson, and ..." turning to the audience "concerned citizens of Alcona County. I was born here – well in Oscoda – and raised there until I went off to school. After college, I joined the Flint Police Force where I served for 25 years and then retired returning here to the most beautiful place on earth or at least I think so."

There was some tittering among the audience.

"As you know, this is not my first attempt to be elected to the office of Sheriff of Alcona County. Actually it is my third campaign and, hopefully my last."

A couple of murmured amens and some tittering from the audience.

"First I want you all to know there is no race involved in this election."

This statement seemed to stun the audience and especially Nathanial and his family. Seeming unconcerned, Leonard continued.

"There is no black or white, just two men vying for one job. I would like to thank my opponent for his good work as deputy sheriff and as acting sheriff."

He nodded to Nathanial and there was modest applause from the audience.

"But ..." and his fist slammed onto the podium – bam "... good isn't good enough. We deserve excellence in the office and that is what I will give."

His yard signs, well spread throughout the county and as prolific as Nathanial's, had white letters on a crimson background:

Elect Hilbreth
Alcona Sheriff
Excellence in Office

explained his emphasis.

"We need better cruisers, better equipment, better pay, and more officers. That is what I will promise you. As well, I will promise you a competent job ... something Nathanial Jefferson has not given you."

There was loud murmuring from the audience and a look of consternation and disbelief on Nathanial's face.

"No, my friends, Nathanial Jefferson has botched the investigation into the perch pond body from the very beginning. Rather than use trained deputies to examine the crime scene and discover evidence, he used untrained and inept citizens, possibly contaminating any evidence."

From the audience there was uncomfortable rustling and even a soft boo or two. Leonard didn't appear to have heard them.

"And what has the sheriff done since then?" He looked out at the audience. "What has he done? Nothing ..." his fist slammed on the podium - bam "...absolutely nothing. Has there been an identification? No!" Bam! "Has there been an arrest? No!" Bam!

"That poor girl's body lies in some laboratory down at State unburied. No rest for her soul. I promise you that I will give that soul the eternal rest that it deserves. I will discover her identity and I will find her killer."

The audience was silent.

"Thank you."

There was loud applause as Leonard Hilbreth took his seat.

Ellen McGinty, a look of slight consternation on her face, stepped to the podium.

"We now have five minutes for questions."

Several hands shot into the air including Dugal's. Ellen McGinty pointed to a man on the other side of the room.

The man rose and said, "This is for both men. Have either of you ever been cited for excellence in the carrying out of your duties as law enforcement officers?"

Dugal thought this question an obvious plant based upon Hilbreth's campaign slogan. Before the question was finished, Leonard had gotten to his feet and strode to the microphone.

"I was officer of the year in 1996 and given a medal for meritorious service in 1999."

He returned to his seat, a smug look on his face. Nathanial stepped to the microphone. "No, I have not," he said candidly and returned to his seat.

Hands shot into the air again. Ellen indicated a woman on the other side closer to the back.

"This is for Sheriff Jefferson. Your opponent has cited needs of the department and says he will see that these needs are met. You made no such statement. Why?"

Nathanial stood up but did not go to the podium. His voice was confident and strong and there was no need for a microphone.

"Yes, we have needs just as Mr. Hilbreth has said. But times are tough, as we all know. Money is tight. I could give you a long list of things that we need, things that Sheriff Collins and I have told the trustees that we need. I can't promise that they will be obtained during my term of office so I won't. All I can do is to promise to run the office and the department to the best of my ability."

He sat down and hands shot into the air. Ellen indicated Dugal who rose.

"Sheriff, Mr. Hilbreth has said that your handling of the perch pond discovery was unorthodox in that civilians were used rather than trained professionals. Why did you do that?"

Again Nathanial stood but this time he went to the podium. "When I saw that a number of trained professionals were needed, I turned to the State Police Crime Lab in Grayling. My department is small and many of them were involved in patrols or in court. I did get the three night deputies to come in but that was not enough. Captain Williamson sent a couple of forensic techs to help but it was going to take a while for them to get here. The Alpena State Police Post could not offer help either. Several men were sick and the six patrolmen from the day watch were involved in a big accident north of city. Captain Williamson suggested the use of the people who were there as long as the work was supervised and evidence logged correctly he felt there was no problem. It was not as though we had discovered a bloody murder in someone's home.

"I followed his suggestion, even to the point of deputizing the men who helped if only to make them be a bit more respectful of the process. Two of the men helped Rich Walker who uncovered the rest of the skeleton and three helped to keep the curious away. Volunteers worked only until official replacements arrived.

"I will admit this was a little unorthodox but I felt that I had no choice. The weather forecast called for heavy rain the next day and with the skeleton partially unearthed, the rain could have washed away parts of it as well as any possible telltale evidence. And, for once, the weather forecast was correct..."

An expected titter ran through the audience and Dugal felt some of the tension he sensed in both Nathanial and the audience ebb.

"...the rain that started early in the night was a really gully washer. I walked in to the dam site early the next morning because there was so much water I didn't want to risk getting stuck. The water had broken through the cofferdam we had built and the stream running through the trench would have washed away part of the skeleton. And I will add that other than the skeleton and the pieces of the plastic bag, nothing was found.

"As for making progress much beyond identifying the sex and relative age of the deceased and obtaining a rendering of how she looked, I will admit there has been no progress."

Murmurs ran through the audience.

"But it has not been for lack of trying. Once we knew that the skeleton was that of a child, we had help from the National Center for Missing and Exploited Children. A member of Team Adam was with us for a week. A DNA sample was obtained but there was no match found with those available samples of missing children. The facial reconstruction was done by them. We have searched records for missing children and have found no match. We have posters out and have posted our information online. All other avenues of approach have led to a dead end. We need someone to come forward with some information. Without more to go on, we are at a dead end. But that doesn't mean we are quitting. We never quit."

Nathanial turned and took his seat. Hands shot into the air.

"Our time for questions has ended. I am sorry but we must stick to the guidelines laid down for tonight. I would like to thank our candidates for their time and you for your interest. Good evening."

The audience applauded and there were shoots of "Good job", "Thank you" as coats were put on and people started moving toward the door at the rear. Dugal noticed that Nathanial exited the stage moving away from Hilbreth without saying anything. He and Earleen didn't wait to talk to him but followed the crowd out the door.

Chapter 24

The wire cage affixed to the downstream side of the earthen dam was aswim with small perch. For the past week the oaken boards in the guillotine gate had been pulled one or two at a time to lower the level of the pond. Now only four remained to be pulled and it was obvious that the removal of each board would bring a large number of perch minnows into the cage.

"Good job, George," everyone was saying to Mr. Warmth and he just nodded and muttered to himself. He and Jim Winchell had installed the cage and had kept a constant check on it.

There were probably thirty sportsmen there that morning to help transfer the perch from the pond to the lake. Everyone had brought coolers, pails, five gallon buckets – anything that could hold water. The DNR had even permitted Richard Hanson, the DNR biologist who had Hibbard Pond in his purview, to bring the DNR truck that was used to carry fish to stock lakes and ponds. He had warned Ed Stockwell that this would probably not be enough if there were a large quantity of perch.

Everything was in readiness or at least as ready as they could be. George and Jim stood at opposite ends of the cage, ready to start scooping fish out. It was a chilly fall morning and everyone was dressed accordingly with sweatshirts advertising an assortment of organizations, colleges or just bearing brazen statements. Most of them had thought to wear waterproof boots and pants; some had simply worn their waders.

Dick Hanson was up on the truck with the lid off the first of two tanks which he had brought filled with water. Because the tanks would be drained when the perch were put into the lake, this method would probably be used at most once. Dick checked to be certain that the aerators were on, and then said, "Let the netting begin."

Jim and George scooped their nets into the water and emerged about a quarter full of perch fingerlings. George passed his net to Ed Stockwell who handed it to Dick and the first of the perch went into the tank. There was a cheer from the assemblage and the stocking process had begun. After four netfuls by each were emptied in the truck with the last two being basically empty, George waved to Rob McIntosh who stood atop the dam.

"Bring up the next board."

Rob hurried across the top of the dam and looked down into the guillotine access pipe where his brother Roy waited.

"Let's pull a board, Roy," Rob said as he grabbed hold of the reinforcing rod hook that his brother had already inserted into the eye of the board's hook. He gave a mighty yank and nothing happened.

"A little help here," he shouted.

Dugal and Jerry had been standing on top of the dam out of the way of the watery mayhem they expected to occur and hurried to help. Each of the three got a good grip on the rod.

"On three," Rob said to them and Roy. "ONE, TWO, THREEEE."

With combined strength of the three of them and Roy pulling below was no match for the water pressure that had previously refused to let the board budge and it yielded, sliding upward six inches. The water gushed through the opening almost knocking Roy off his feet. He would have fallen except for the tight quarters.

The three gatekeepers let go of the rod and hurried across the dam to see the water spurting into the cage. By the time they reached the downstream side, George and Jim each had swiped their nets into the cage and returned a quarter full of perch. For the next fifteen minutes things were fast and furious and both tanks of the DNR tanker had been filled. Dick put the lids on the tanks, made certain that the aerators were on and waved goodbye as he started the truck for the south end of the lake where the perch would be released at the Negwegon Township Launch Site at the south end of the lake. The various containers would take the remainder of the perch to the Loon Creek DNR Launch Site, which was considerably closer.

Work then got a little sloppier. Buckets were filled with water, perch dumped in and two, three, four buckets a vehicle and they headed for the lake. With no aeration time was of the essence. Things became a little more reserved however when the first of these stocking vehicles returned. Bill and Tess Worthington—she being one of the few women who had shown up—returned with a sad but hilarious story. They had fastened three buckets in place using bungee cords and driven hell bent for leather for the Loon Creek Launch Site. They had pulled up and hurried to the rear of their pickup to get the buckets of perch into the lake. The sight that greeted them was anything but glorious. The three five gallon buckets, each of which was almost full, were over half empty and the contents, at least the non-liquid portion, was spread across the bed of the pickup. Most of the fingerlings, two to three inches long, were flopping around the bed but some were just lying there. Tess's fast thinking saved many of them. She had gotten into the truck and backed down the ramp until the rear wheels were in the lake. She had been shouting instructions at Bill, who then lowered the gate and they literally swept the perch into the lake using a push broom that Bill also kept handy to sweep out to the truck's bed from a load of whatever. The remains of the three buckets were emptied into the lake. They had been fearful that the lake resident sea gulls would get wind of things and swoop in to help themselves but by the time they headed back to the pond the sky was clear. Not so, reported the next returnees. A feast was being made of the dead and almost dead perch that could not make it into deep water. Fortunately seagulls are top feeders unlike their invasive cousins the cormorants.

Things slowed down then and buckets were only half full and speeds were held down to prevent spillage. Two SUVS arrived just prior to noon, each bearing two or three Sportsman wives and, better than that, a homemade lunch of chili, hot dogs, chips, assorted condiments and other fixings. Most appreciated was a cooler of beer and pop. Platefuls were handed to the hungry and grateful workers who found seats on car bumpers, truck beds, or the side of the dam.

"Uh-oh, here comes trouble," George Jamison said. Everyone within earshot looked where he was pointing and saw a sheriff's SUV bumping down the path, lights flashing. From that moment on, there was utter silence as the sheriff's SUV pulled up. The lights went off, the door opened and Nathanial got out. Ed Stockwell started toward him but stopped when Nathanial raised his hand. He bent into his SUV and emerged bearing a box.

"I am willing to share this box of several dozen of Gert's double chocolate walnut brownies just out of the oven for a plateful of lunch."

And share they did. Dugal found the opportunity to talk to Nathanial before he left.

"You scared the bejesus out of us coming down that road with lights flashing. We thought there was another body."

Nathanial's smiled from ear to ear, "Well, those brownies are best eaten warm and I had to clear a path."

Afterward the rest of the boards were pulled, the last of the perch netted and taken to the lake. George Jamison and Jim Winchell removed the cage and carried it to a high spot by some trees where it would remain until the next time the pond was drained. Rob and Roy got the boards back into the guillotine gate. Ed Stockwell thanked everyone and the sportsmen headed home, another job well done but with the usual minor catastrophes. As Ed said, "If there aren't a couple of screw-up's, then it's not a successful Sportsman function."

Chapter 25

The early morning light glistened off the frosted red, orange and yellow leaves. Gill could see his breath in front of him as though he was smoking, which he had tried once or twice. But smoking and hunting were not things that mixed well together. Smoke – especially tobacco smoke – indicated "man" and no deer would stay long in an area where man was. Especially not in the early fall when the rut was in bloom and deer seemed to know that man would be in the woods.

Side-to-side Gill let his eyes move. Just his eyes – nothing else – because any movement might startle a deer. His older brother Ken had told him that once after three hours sitting on the stand, he had moved his leg just a bit to ease a cramp. He had been startled by the crashing of brush and caught a glimpse of a white tail as a six-point buck had vanished from his sight. Somehow the buck had walked into his line of vision and had stood there – Ken didn't know for how long. The buck had stood there – a twenty-yard shot if Ken had noticed it. But the buck had been nearly invisible in the twilight of dawn. This was a mistake that Gill, on his first hunt alone, was determined not to make.

The snort startled Gill and he started to turn his head but held himself still. Somewhere to his left was a deer. Gill's eyes held tightly left and then quickly scanned the area in front of him. On the movement to the right, he canvassed the area immediately in front and on the return the area further away toward the orchard. It wasn't really an orchard, just four apple trees that his father had planted in the clearing near the pond over twenty years ago. Four apple trees carefully pruned and sprayed each year. Four apple trees that produced the choicest of apples, very few of which were eaten by man. Four apple trees that produced the choicest of apples that were eaten only by deer. Four apple trees that produced an average of two deer a year for the Fisher family. Four apple trees that provided a natural bait area proving his father's wisdom now that the DNR had banned baiting in this part of the state.

His eyes paused as they passed the orchard. Nothing there. The scan continued until the eyes were locked left. Something was different – a slight movement. Stillness. What it was Gill couldn't see? Nervousness caused another scan. He sensed the fingers of his left hand tightening on the bow, the fingers of his right hand, impatiently tightening, yearning to draw the arrow back. Nothing in front, right or in the orchard. On the left another movement but this time not unknown. The slightly brightening dawn had glistened off something. Gill squinted trying to force his eyes to magnify and draw the object in.

Antlers – moving ever so slightly. As his vision cleared his breath caught. It was the biggest buck that Gill had ever seen. Ten or twelve points at least, maybe even bigger. The buck was looking around, smelling the air. The slight morning breeze was not coming from behind him and Gill knew that he would not be sensed. But any sudden movement and the buck would be gone. Yet he had to start his draw.

The buck took a step down the trodden path made by he and others of his kind. The path that would take him – as it had time and time again – through the orchard to the spring that gurgled on the other side. The same spring that had motivated Gill's father to plant those four apple trees those twenty odd years before. The buck continued his slow patient journey toward the orchard. Gill's bow continued its slow journey to the fully drawn position – a journey practiced time and time again first under the training regimen of his father and later by himself. A journey practiced often as he sat in his tree stand during the summer months time and time again training himself to be patient. His movement stopped when the buck did or when the buck's gaze, constantly moving as Gill's had, was in his direction. Gill knew that the buck would have to look up to see him, twenty feet up to where Gill sat on his stand in that massive red oak. But any movement was warning, warning of danger, and the buck would be off.

Finally, after an eternity it seemed to Gill even though he had done this many times before, the buck paused under the spreading limbs of a red delicious apple tree. His head turned side-to-side, he sniffed the air, seemed to tense ... and then relaxed. Almost as though it had been holding its breath and had exhaled. The tautness appear to relax, the deer relaxed, dropped his guard ever so slightly as he lowered his head to get one of the apples lying on the ground.

That movement of relaxation was Gill's key – his arrow was fully drawn – his aim seemed true. He held his breath, steadied his hands, and released his breath and the arrow simultaneously. The buck startled – his head erect, his eyes blazing. Then he was gone – disappearing into the woods to the right of the orchard. Gill could hear the departure but couldn't believe it. This was a shot he had practiced here all summer. He knew the distance. He knew the height. He knew the spot. How could he have missed? The slight twang of the bow relaxing as the arrow released – the warning couldn't have been in time. The arrow had appeared to fly true.

Gill waited cursing to himself as he heard the buck vanish. He sat still for several minutes. Then he tied the bow to the rope and lowered it to the ground. He released his safety belt and slowly stood up welcoming the message of pain that his cramped muscles sent. He held onto the tree as he waited for the pain to subside. The blood rushed through once constricted vessels and in a minute he was fine. He swung himself onto the ladder and started down. Then he climbed the few steps back to the stand and picked up his backpack, put it over his arms, and once again started down the tree.

On the ground he retrieved his bow and walked to the orchard. The apple with one bite gone lay on the ground, steam slowly rising from its freshly opened warmth. Gill stared at the ground, searching the area for any sign of blood – there was none. He walked past the tree toward the spring looking for the arrow. He didn't find it. After ten minutes of looking Gill was satisfied that he hadn't missed. The arrow was in the deer but off target. Maybe it had hit a bone and veered away from the heart. The only way he would ever know was to find the deer.

Before he could do that he had to let Ken know he was out of the stand and tracking. He pulled the cell phone from his belt and punched Ken's speed dial button. Two rings and he hit stop, counted to twenty, as he knew Ken was doing and redialed. Two rings and he stopped, put the phone back on his belt and started tracking his deer. He knew that Ken was counting to twenty, waiting for his phone to vibrate again. That would mean the deer was down. It was their prearranged code. If Gill had been in trouble, he would have let the phone continue to ring on the first call and Ken would have answered.

Fortunate to have seen the deer depart, the early tracking was easy but Gill moved slowly, his eyes searching the ground, the leaves, the rocks, the trees for any sign that the deer had been hit. The telltale drops of dark red blood on the brown leaves was a welcome sight but they were few and scattered. For forty-five minutes Gill pressed onward traveling well over a mile uncertain that he was still following the buck but following something, of that he was certain.

He came to the edge of a thicket of cedars. He knew he was well off his father's property, not really certain where he was because he had been so intent on the tracking. His heart seemed to stop and his breath caught in his throat as the sound of a truck's engine reached his ears. He searched the area around him and then through the trees and some forty or fifty feet up and maybe a hundred yards away he spotted movement. It was then he realized where his was. The north side of the Comrock S-curve. He was on Big Stag Club property.

His thoughts quickly returned to the deer and he started into the thicket and stopped. Something yellow in one of the trees caught his eye. He moved the branches and saw it, his arrow with a yellow shank, blue fletching with green cock feather and bronze nock. He retrieved it and looked at the broad head – dark red in contrast with the silver metal. He had hit the deer but how badly he still didn't know. His eyes alert for the slightest sign, he pushed into the thicket.

Half an hour earlier and he wouldn't have been able to see a thing but the sun was now up and shining brightly. Inside the thicket was a small clearing – about three by eight feet, the ground covered with dead fronds and branches and something else. There was a slight bump in the center of the clearing. The ground seemed to rise about six inches into a narrow mound about four feet long and a foot or so wide. The floor covering at one side of the mound had been disturbed as the deer went through and something was poking up from the ground. Gill stooped down and brushed the forest debris away – it was blue and had a rusted metal eyelet in it. It was a piece of plastic tarp.

Curious Gill grasped the tarp and tugged. It gave a little. He pulled harder and the earth seemed to give and the tarp came slightly free. Gill pulled harder but couldn't budge the corner. He moved to the other side of the mound, grasped the tarp and pulled again. Nothing. He braced his feet, grasped the tarp, took a deep breath and pulled.

He found himself sitting against the trunk of one of the cedars. The tarp corner was laying on his legs and ... the smell! He looked in front of him seeing dirt and another corner of the tarp lying about his ankles. He reached out and flipped it back away from him. The sight caused him to shut his eyes and scream. Then the full force of the smell made him turn on his side and wretch. After a minute he got his cell phone from his belt and pressed Ken's number. This time he let it ring.

Chapter 26

Mitchell Webster was the first law enforcement officer to arrive on the scene. He had been patrolling Hibbard Pond Path and was only five minutes away from the S-curve when the call went out. He had turned his patrol car around and started the flashers as he sped toward the S-curve. Mitchell had been with the Hibbard County sheriff's department for only three months having joined upon graduation from Wayne Community College with a two-year degree in law enforcement. His only experience had been with traffic violators, except for the body in the perch pond which had been discovered only a week after he joined the force.

From the radio dispatcher, he knew that a teenager had claimed to have discovered a body in a shallow grave in a cedar copse on the north side of the S-curve. That was all that Ken Willis had gotten from his brother when he answered his hysterical call. He had put his younger brother on hold and called 911 with the basic information. He had clambered down from his stand a quarter mile from Gill's and set out to find him, simultaneously talking to him. Gill hadn't even realized that Ken had put him on hold and was just repeating the same information over and over again. Ken realized that Gill was in shock and he was doing his best to get to him as quickly as possible. Using Gill's cell phone number, the dispatcher had run a GPS trace and radioed his location to Mitchell and all available units.

Mitchell pulled off the road next to the guardrail in the middle of the S-curve and called out – there was no response. His eyes swept the terrain and he noticed several clusters of cedars – one of which held his quarry. Turning on his lights, he grabbed a couple of flares and walked back toward the south end of the S-curve putting one every 50 feet to warn oncoming traffic that something was blocking the road ahead. Then he half walked, half slid down the fifty-foot embankment and

123

headed toward the nearest copse, breaking his way through the brush. As he neared it, he realized that it wasn't the one he wanted as he could see through and nothing was there. He headed deeper into the trees. As he neared the third cedar grove, he realized that this was the one he wanted. Two things, a voice and a smell, had alerted his senses. Both were faint but each strengthened as he neared.

" ... in a tarp under the trees ... rotten ... human ... dead ... covered with dirt ... I pulled the tarp ... help me, Ken please ..."

Mitchell called out but there was no answer and he pushed his way into the trees and his senses were assaulted – the smell of rotting flesh would forever remain embedded in his memory. His stomach seemed to turn inside out and bile assaulted his throat. If he had been alone, he would have given in but the sight of Gill and the innate knowledge that help was needed steeled his body and he fought back the feeling of nausea.

Gill was still sitting with his back to the tree, his cell phone held carelessly, it seemed, against his cheek and he continued his rambling. His eyes were sightless and stared straight at and through Mitchell ... unseeing, uncomprehending. Mitchell didn't realize until later what guided his own actions at that point. It was only several hours later when he had time to sit and relax that he was able to understand his actions. It wasn't his law enforcement training – none of it had prepared him for this. It was his Boy Scout training, especially knowledge and practical work gained from earning his first aid merit badge that guided his actions. He realized that Gill was in shock and needed immediate attention, which he could not get here.

He crossed the short distance to Gill, picked him up, and pushed his way through the trees. Almost as soon as he cleared the branches Gill seemed to relax. His eyes closed, his arm dropped, his hand opened, and the cell phone, still on, fell to the ground. Mitchell was fortunate that Gill took after his father rather than his mother as Ken did. Gill at five feet nine, weighed less than one hundred pounds whereas Ken, two years older, was six feet one and weighed 250.

At the bottom of the bank, Mitchell put Gill over his shoulder so that he would have one hand free to assist his ascent. The steep bank was covered with deep grass, saplings and small bushes, which Mitchell used to help pull himself up the hill. Half crawling, often sliding back, he struggled upward. Despite the coolness of the morning, he was quickly drenched with sweat. He was ready to collapse halfway up the hill, when hands reached out and took Gill from him. Hands and voices tried to reassure him but Mitchell slumped to the ground as his previous nausea returned and racked his body. The two first responder members of the Hibbard Pond Rescue Squad left Mitchell and carried Gill the rest of the way up the hill. They started first aid once they laid him on the stretcher inside their vehicle. Theirs was the second vehicle to arrive at the scene to be followed only moments later by the sheriff, a state patrol cruiser, and five trucks containing other first responders who were also members of the sheriff's search and rescue squad.

Chapter 27

Nathanial dispatched some of the members of his squad to secure the area once he had ascertained its position from Mitchell already learning that he would not gain very much information from Gill for a while. He clambered down the bank and stood below Mitchell who was now sitting up, his head between his legs.

"That bad, huh?" Nathanial queried.

Mitchell's reply was just a shake of his head.

"I can remember my first encounter with a ripe one. I was in my second year..." Nathanial was stopped in his story by Mitchell's glare.

"Okay, now that I've got your attention, Deputy Webster. Where's the body?"

"About seventy five yards straight back from the bottom of the hill. Big group of red cedar. You'll know by the smell."

"Not if VapoRub works like it used to," Nathanial said. "Better get some to carry in your patrol car. Meanwhile use mine; it's on the front seat. Pull yourself together and then join me."

Nathanial turned and started down the hill when Ken burst out of the woods.

"Where's Gill?" He blurted, bending over with his hands on his knees and gasping for breath.

"Up in the ambulance," Nathanial responded. "I surprised that the coach doesn't have you in better shape. It's the middle of the season and you act like you haven't done anything other than run a mile or so through the woods."

Ken was too busy trying to catch his breath to respond. Ken was a second string guard on the Saginaw Valley football team and had taken advantage of a bye in the schedule to come home for the opening day of bow season. He was fortunate that the coach was also a hunter and was also taking advantage of the bye, which he had thoughtfully established in the schedule.

He understood that hunting was a large part of the life for many of the members of his team. To have kept them on campus for opening day would have caused a major rebellion and with a 5-1 record, 4-0 in the conference, he could not afford that. As he had once said to the press, "You can take the boy out of the woods but you can't take the woods out of the boy."

Nathanial turned and headed for the woods, leaving Ken to struggle up the hill and point out the direction to members of the rescue squad who were now coming to join the sheriff. Several of the team had joined him by the time he reached the copse and he instructed them on the size of the perimeter he wanted.

Then he made his way into the copse. The VapoRub worked for the most part, at least to camouflage the smell somewhat. The body was hard to describe part except for size. Although two corners of the tarp had been removed there was still the other two, one of which laid about the knee area and the other down to the middle of the chest and covering the head.

Nathanial permitted himself one quick look and then retreated, waiting until his forensics team would arrive to photograph and search the area for any evidence. He knew from experience that the body had been there for a while, several months at least. Familiar with the area, he realized that whoever had put the body here had done so intentionally and with great effort because there were no roads in this part of the Big Stag Club Property and Hibbard Pond Path was the closest. This meant carrying the body down the hill and then about the seventy-five yards to this spot.

Of course the body could have been dragged in the tarp or maybe the person was alive and had gotten to this point under his or her own power, only to end life here for whatever reason. Nathanial pulled out his phone and dialed the office.

"Barbara Ann, we've definitely got a body here. Appears to be a youngster but that is just a guess. Been here for a while. Guess you better start searching for missing juveniles – actually any missing people in the area – from the spring forward."

He listened to his dispatcher for a moment.

"Yes, I know we did that this past spring but that was missing girls ten years ago. Now I want missing kids, both sexes, from this past spring. And that might be just a start."

He listened again.

"Yes, and check that missing kids website. National Center for Missing and Exploited Children – Google it."

His forensic team of Rich Walker and Bob Roberts arrived within fifteen minutes and set about their work. Half an hour later a State Police cadaver sniffing dog arrived and started searching the woods around the cedar copse. It was early enough in the day that after a few hours the dog was done. No other bodies discovered but he didn't expect there to be. The forensic team was done about the same time having not discovered anything substantial. Some smudged fingerprints but nothing good enough to use. The body was ready to be removed and taken to the Blodgett Medical Facility in Grand Rapids for further investigation.

He pulled out his cell phone and made the necessary call.

"Hibbard Pond Funeral Home. Wallace Hibbs speaking. May I be of service?"

"Sheriff Jefferson here, Wallace. We have a body in the woods on the north side of the S-Curve that needs to be removed."

"You are certainly the purveyor of bad tidings, aren't you, Nathanial. Is this a car accident?"

"No, it's a ripe one found wrapped in a tarp in a cedar copse about one hundred yards from the north side of the S-curve."

"You don't make them easy, do you?"

"We'll get the body up to the south side of the curve. You bring your hearse down and take it from there. We'll need to get it down to Grand Rapids as soon as possible."

"Will tomorrow do? I have calling hours tonight and funeral the day after up in Alpena."

"No problem, Wallace. We'll have the body up in about thirty minutes."

"I'll be there."

That checked off his list, of course there were the press and the gawkers. After the original arrival of his people, all vehicles had been moved to the south end of the S-curve where a broad grassy area was available. It was difficult to get the passing motorists to keep moving because it was obvious that something was happening. Those northbound were able to pull completely off the road just north of the curve and those southbound parked with one wheel off the road. The crowd gathered on the side opposite of the site and his men were able to keep them there. The press was there, the Alpena News and Channel 11, and a freelance reporter who would undoubtedly submit reports to The Alcona Review, the Flint Journal and both Detroit newspapers. If he was lucky, he would be in food for a month.

Nathanial knew he would have to say something. It would be obvious that there was a body – you couldn't hide that being carried up the slope. And there was the ambulance which had taken Gill to the hospital just for observation and treatment for shock. One of his officers had taken Ken to his car. Sooner or later he would have to make a statement and what better time than now and maybe ease the removal of the body.

He climbed the steep slope he had come down before rather than the sloping path of the drain creek that the litter carriers would use. He stopped at the guardrail and looked across the street noting that most of the crowd had moved up opposite the parking area when the ambulance had arrived. He crossed the guardrail and the street waving to Officer Webster who was helping to keep the crowd orderly. Most of them were senior citizens it being the middle of the week and most young men were in the woods on opening day of bow season. Mitchell waved back just as he hoped he would and Nathanial started walking slowly toward the crowd. The press noticed the wave by Mitchell; saw the sheriff and started to converge followed slowly by most of the crowd. Nathanial waved to Mitchell to come along and continued walking.

He met the press halfway and to afford a better venue, he climbed the slight bank on the other side of the drainage ditch. The press gathered seemingly at his feet, the TV camera rolling, camera flashes illuminating him in the shadows cast by the trees in the early afternoon sun, reporters shooting questions. He held up his hand and the crowd quieted.

"Shortly after eight o'clock this morning, my office received a call from a young hunter who reported that his brother had found a body in a copse of cedars but his didn't know where. He gave us his brother's cell phone number and we used GPS tracking to locate the phone. Officer Webster," and he indicated Mitchell "was the first officer on the scene and he climbed down the hill and found the boy. He brought the boy up the hill where first responders administered first aid – the lad was just suffering from shock – and removed him to Alpena General. The boy's name is Gill Fisher and he was hunting with his brother Ken, who plays football for Saginaw Valley. I am certain that in a couple of days Gill will feel like making a statement but I ask you to please wait until my office gives you the okay so that we can talk to him first."

Nathanial knew that an officer was already waiting at the hospital to do that but also knew that Gill would need his privacy now and his fifteen minutes of fame later, although Nathanial was certain that he would wish his fame had come some other way. He could see the litter carriers nearing the top of the hill and then Wallace's grey and black hearse eased past but not unnoticed.

"We don't know anything about the person whose body …"

A member of the press with some sixth sense no doubt had seen the litter nearing the top of the hill just before the hearse passed and the press broke flowing behind the hearse, Mitchell hard pressed to keep up with them. They streamed across the street seemingly oblivious to the semi that was proceeding northbound slowly through the curve, its driver gawking at the scene, ignoring the hearse until the press passed in front. Then alert, he blew his horn only to have it ignored. Only the trailers, the curious seniors, gave way for the motorized behemoth and wisely stayed on the south side of the curve.

Nathanial sighed, his press conference over for now, waiting for the semi to creep past, the driver not even noticing him, crossed the street and the guardrail and made his way to the hearse. In addition to the litter bearers, Rich Walker and Bob Roberts had come along and were helping Mitchell Webster keep the press back. Cameras rolling and reporters shouting questions, Wallace Hibbs opened the hearse's door and the litter bearing the body was slid inside. Wallace climbed in and fastened the litter securely and then climbed out, closing the door. The press was kept away by the hearse itself as he walked to the driver's door. The freelancer broke from the group and headed for the front of the vehicle only to be blocked by Nathanial's bulk.

"I would appreciate it, as would Mr. Hibbs, if you would give the deceased a little privacy. Anything you need to know, you can get from my office. Now behave yourself."

Chagrined but quietly muttering obvious epitaphs, the freelancer back off and joined the small throng of reporters who were now filing northward along the guard rail trying to get a view of the site where the body had been discovered. The hearse pulled out and with the help of the officers, was able to back up and head north, slowly passing the press on the north side and the seniors who had remained on the south side. All tried to get a view of what the hearse carried but there wasn't much to see.

Nathanial couldn't help but wonder about the morbid nature of people who gathered to almost revel in the misfortune of others. Shaking his head, he followed his forensics team back to the copse using the easier path the litter had followed this time. With the body removed Rich Walker and Bob Roberts devoted time to the copse where the body had lain. Apparently, a crude shallow grave had been dug; its depth probably limited because of frozen ground and roots was their guess because they presumed the body had been there four to six months. Sheltered in the cedars and the rest of the woods, the ground and body would have taken a long time to thaw accounting for the state of decomposition. Fortunately, for whatever reason, the woodland creatures had been at the body only minimally – for that they had no explanation.

Work on the site continued until late afternoon. All the ground had been covered for quite a distance around the site and was deemed clean. Although the copse was marked off by yellow crime scene tape, Nathanial posted no guard.

As expected, Gill Fisher had nothing of value to add other than his explanation of discovering the body. The arrow he had shot was collected as part of the evidence but blood traces were those only of deer.

Chapter 28

The night the body was discovered local news had full coverage.

Another tragedy in the news tonight from Hibbard Pond. 17-year-old Gill Fisher discovered a partially decomposed body today while tracking a deer. Fisher was hunting alone for the first time today on opening day of Archery Season when he shot a deer from his tree stand. Tracking the deer into a cedar copse near the Comrock S-curve, the young hunter discovered a corpse wrapped in a tarp according to reports.

On the television, the scene shifted from the Channel 11 News @ 6 to show the litter being carried up the hill while Wallace Hibbs waited by his hearse.

Sheriff Jefferson was talking to reporters when the body was carried to the hearse of Hibbard Pond Funeral Home. The body will be taken to Blodgett Medical Facility in Grand Rapids for an autopsy to determine the cause of death and identification. This is the second body to be discovered in the Hibbard Pond area this year. You might remember ...

He remembered and mental images raged through his mind.
Blinding snow with the sick Sue Ellen on the seat beside him. Something in the road. Braking, trying to stop, the skid, tremor as the wheel had come off, teetering on the edge of the

slope for just that moment then sliding down the hill, hitting the bottom ...

Black plastic holding the body of his Sue Ellen. Tears flowing down his cheeks as he had shoveled the dirt on top of her still form in the middle of the night. Then watching from the woods the next morning as the bulldozer pushed more dirt and buried her deeper.

A small cedar casket lowered into the grave beside that of her mother. Tears blinding as he shoveled dirt on top. The small cross next to the big one marking the graves of his beloved Sue Ellen.

He got up from his chair in front of the small black and white television and went to check on Sue Ellen. She was sleeping peacefully in her small bed with her Reggie lying close-by.

Back in his great room he checked the packs he always had ready, made certain that the ammo bag was easily accessible but out of her way. He was ready-he had to be—especially now. He could run now but that would mean leaving his Sue Ellen in her place near the woods and he couldn't do that. Not yet.

*****

It was early the next morning, Nathanial was at his desk catching up when Barbara Ann knocked on his door and entered.

"Yes, Barbara Ann?"

"Rob Colson, Channel 11 news is on line one. He wants to ask some questions about Leonard Hilbreth's statement regarding the S-curve corpse."

"Why can't they leave me alone?" he muttered.

"Goes with the territory, sheriff," Barbara Ann closed the door as Nathanial sighed and picked up the phone.

"Sheriff Jefferson here, what can I do for you, Mr. Colson?"

"I would like some feedback on Leonard Hilbreth's comments about this latest body."

"And precisely what are those?" Nathanial asked because he hadn't heard.

"He claims that this '...second body in five months with no progress made on the first death brings the efficiency and competence of the Alcona County Sheriff's Department into question'."

Nathanial thought for a moment.

"First, it's six months. I admit that we haven't made any headway into identifying the skeleton from the dam but we have utilized all resources at our disposal. With an old death like that one, progress is slow. As for the second one, that was only yesterday and again we are doing everything we can. My officers are out seeking anyone who might know anything. The body is being send to Blodgett Medical Facility in Grand Rapids today and we hope for some help from them but that may take as much as a week."

Silence on the other end of the phone as though Colson was expecting more. Then ...

"That's it?"

"I am sorry, Mr. Colson, but that is all that I can say. As in the case of any mysterious death, there are certain details that we don't give out, details we feel that only the guilty party or parties would know, details that may help identify these people but would alert them if we made the information public.

"Now, if there is nothing else, I have an investigation to continue."

"Thank you, Sheriff," Colson said.

"Any time," Nathanial said.

Chapter 29

The big question facing Nathanial and his force was "How did the body get there?" How the person had died was the province of the Blodgett medical staff. Mitchell Webster was given the task of tracking down the possibility of getting the body there from a vehicle on the S-curve. One thing that people remembered was a semi almost going through the railing in early March and removing the southern half before coming to a halt, its cab over the edge and hanging there only because of the trailer's weight. Winter weather had delayed replacement of the railing until June. That could have provided easier access to the spot. It was a long hike from any road in the Big Stag Club property but snowmobiles were always a possibility.

Mitchell contacted all the local towing companies but none reported any towing at the S-curve since the semi. Thus he expanded his search and finally hit what promised to be of some help. Marcie Miller, wife of Peter Miller who ran Miller's towing out of Posen, recalled a strange call in early May.

"It was the morning after that freak snowstorm in May," she told Mitchell. He got a call from a friend was all he said and went out. He was gone for several hours and when he came back he didn't say much except he had to pull up an old pickup from that Hibbard Pond Path S-curve."

Mitchell learned there was no record of the tow or none that she could find and her husband was in the UP for a week hunting bear and had no cell phone and had left no contact. He went every other year but she didn't know where, was just glad to get rid of him for a week. The forensics team had found indications of a vehicle having gone over the side and being removed but couldn't determine how much was removing the semi or another vehicle.

However the Blodgett medical lab was having more success. The body was that of a young girl, Nathanial cringed when he heard that, but there were no signs of her having died a violent death but the victim had been ailing from flu. A DNA sample had been secured and was being run and when the results were in they would be run through all databases seeking a match.

The results when they came back were shocking. Jennifer Duncan was three and a half years old when abducted from a parked car in a shopping mall parking lot five years ago. She had been the winner of Miss Baby Michigan, a one-time small pageant that had spread her photo in newspapers and television across the state. Her mother was running errands and Jennifer had fallen asleep. Having just to run into a jewelry store and drop something off, her mother had left Jennifer in the car. When she came back in five minutes – it may have been ten, she admitted – Jennifer was gone.

Nathanial was unable to comprehend why a mother would leave a child unattended in a parking lot, especially in an unlocked car. No one had seen anything. An AMBER Alert had been sounded but there never was a confirmed sighting. One sighting had her in Traverse City, a second in Holland, and one in Standish. That made Nathanial take notice because Standish is just off I-75 and is the interstate one takes in getting from Detroit to Hibbard Pond or at least as close as you can get on an interstate. The National Center for Missing and Exploited Children had her picture at the time of her disappearance.

Included with the report was the contact information for the parents and a reconstructed picture of her as she looked now at age eight and a half. But that was not needed, the DNA was enough. The picture would be shown around to see if anyone recognized her but Nathanial didn't have much faith in that.

While it was probably better to make a notification like this in person and that would have been the responsibility of the State Police or the police in the Detroit suburb of Huntington Woods where her parents still lived, Nathanial wanted to do it himself. So he called the number and waited through ten rings for either one of the parents or an answering machine to pick up but there was no answer. And there was no answer to Nathanial's other question: What is the relationship between Jennifer Duncan and the girl in the perch pond?

Chapter 30

M-72 is a state of Michigan highway from Harrisville on Lake Huron to the community of Empire in the Sleeping Bear Dunes National Lakeshore on Lake Michigan. It is one of only three highways to cross Michigan's Lower Peninsula, shore to shore. The designation M means that it is a state highway differentiating it from county designated roads like F-41 that crosses M-72 just west of Lincoln. There are 7 zones labeled A-H with G and H being in the Upper Peninsula and the F designation encompassing the upper east side of the Lower Peninsula including Alcona County. The only U.S. highway to run through the county is U.S. 23 that runs up the east side of the county through Harrisville.

It was a sunny fall afternoon that found Nathanial sitting in his cruiser in a rest area on the north side of M-72 just a little west of where it tops a hill. Once a car crested the hill the cruiser was in plain sight but by then it was too late as it was for the black Cadillac Escalade that registered 85 m.p.h., thirty miles above the legal limit, on Nathanial's hand held radar gun. Nathanial didn't need the gun to know that the driver had applied the brakes as soon as he spotted him.

"At least he isn't going to run," Nathanial thought as he entered the SUV's license number into his computer and then pulled out behind the vehicle. He glanced at the display and saw that the vehicle had a previous ticket on this same road the previous year. *"Points really mounting up,"* Nathanial thought as he turned on his flashers and the SUV immediately pulled over. Nathanial took his time getting out and as he stood up he made certain that his pistol was unencumbered in case he needed it although he didn't think he would.

Walking up next to the vehicle, Nathanial noticed that the window was rolled down and he felt the blast of cold air from the air conditioning.

"Would you please turn your engine off, sir," Nathanial said.

The driver complied after slight hesitation.

"Do you know how fast you were going, sir," Nathanial said.

"Too fast I guess, Sheriff," was the reply.

"Yes, sir, you were thirty miles over the speed limit."

"Couldn't have been more than fifteen," was the man's reply.

"Can I see your license and vehicle registration, please," responded Nathanial ignoring the man's innuendo.

"Here," and the man passed the papers through the window. Looking through them Nathanial observed some money folded in thirds so that it fitted neatly behind the license.

He held it up to the driver.

"What's this, sir?"

"A contribution to your campaign fund, Sheriff. Been meaning to do it."

Nathanial nodded wondering what he would have said if he hadn't been running for office.

"That's quite generous of you, Mr. Breckenridge, but I can't accept donations directly. They might get misconstrued as a bribe and we won't want that. Would we, Mr. Breckenridge?"

"No, we wouldn't, Sheriff," the man said and Nathanial could sense him starting to simmer.

He handed the money back to the man with a card he kept attached to his clipboard for just such an occasion.

"Here's one of my campaign cards that gives you the address to which you can send the donation or a number to call and one of the volunteers will come to get it. I'll just be a minute, sir."

Nathanial said and then turned and walked back to his car. He sat in the seat and wrote out the ticket double-checking the information to be certain that it was accurate. Then, ticket book in hand he walked back to the car that was already idling but he said nothing. He handed the ticket, license and registration papers to the driver.

"You can send in the amount listed within the next week and not have to make a court appearance or you can call the number and set up a court date if you wish to appeal.

"Do you have any questions, sir?"

"No," was the sullen reply.

"Have a nice day, sir, and drive safely."

Nathanial turned and started back toward his cruiser.

"Say goodbye to your donation and my vote, you black sonnovabitch."

Nathanial whirled and walked back to the driver's window. Bending down he looked the driver in the face, "Did I just hear a racial slur, sir? Because if I did it ...."

The driver glared at him, put the SUV in gear and sped off leaving a plume of black exhaust and tire marks in the shoulder's gravel. Nathanial stared after him and decided that continuing the confrontation wasn't worth it.

Just as he reached his cruiser, he heard the whirrr of the rumble strip on the road and looked across the road to see a shabby pickup truck pulling back on the road from where it had apparently gone off onto the shoulder. The correction was too much as the truck crossed the double yellow line and its rumble strip and then pulled back just before a van loaded with a vacationing family from Wisconsin crested the hill headed west. A moment earlier, Nathanial thought, and he would have been in the middle of horrific head-on collision. Getting into his cruiser he checked his rearview mirror and the road ahead before executing a U-turn and taking off after the pickup, lights ablaze. Cresting the hill eastbound he watched the pickup make another entrance back on the road from the right shoulder again crossing the double yellow before another correction took it back into its lane heading again for the shoulder. Nathanial picked up speed, added his siren to his lights and pulled up behind the pickup. This continued for half a mile before the pickup's brake lights came on and the truck rolled to a stop only about half on the shoulder. Nathanial pulled up behind the truck, checked his rearview mirror and then exited his cruiser, striding rapidly to the pickup's door.

A red-faced grungy bearded Gabby Hayes countenance greeted him. The driver peered at him through half open eyes and a smile of rotten teeth.

"S'matter, ossifer. Lost?"

"No, sir, I am not. How about you, sir. Can you drive?"

"Course I can – s'why I'm here. Driving myself home."

"Well can you pull ahead a little and get completely off the road so you don't get hit by someone who can't drive as well as you."

"Certainly. Glads to do it."

The man put the truck into gear as Nathanial stepped away and the truck pulled forward onto the road and continued east, heading first for the double yellow. Nathanial raced for his cruiser, throwing into gear, hitting the siren, and taking off after the truck. Other drivers were pulling off the road as they should have but it was over as mile before the brake lights on the pickup flashed, the left turn indicator went on and the truck pulled onto the right shoulder and rolled to a stop well off the road this time.

Quickly Nathanial was at the driver's door.

"S'matter, ossifer? Lost?" came from the rotten toothed grin.

"Would you get out of the truck please, sir," Nathanial said.

"Certainly, ossifer. Just as soon as I can get belted."

"You already are," Nathanial thought, *"but I have to be sure."*

It took Jake Bellows five minutes to get the seatbelt undone (*"At least he was wearing one,"* Nathanial thought) and then he opened the door, got out and fell flat on his face. Rolling over, with blood running out of his nose, he said "Ossifer, I've fallen and can't get up" and then he laughed or rather cackled ending in a cough. Using the truck's running board, seat and door handles, Jake finally made it up.

"Can't help him," Nathanial reminded himself. *"Look too suspicious."*

So he stood and watched, as did the passers-by who gawked at the proceedings obviously alerted to something by the cruiser's flashing lights. Finally Jake was up and Nathanial asked him to walk to the front of the truck, which Jake managed to do after closing the truck's door and using its handle and the fender to stay upright.

"Can't ask him to walk a straight line, he'll fall down for certain."

Once at the front of the truck, Nathanial motioned him forward and Jake hesitantly took a teetering step and then stood there like a flag blowing in the wind.

"Okay, Jake," Nathanial said "Hold your arms out to the side."

Nathanial stuck his out as an illustration. Jake stuck out one, dropped it and then the other and dropped it.

"No, both at the same time like me."

It took three tries but Jake managed.

"Okay, now watch me. Close your eyes and touch your right index finger to your nose and then your left."

Demonstration done, Nathanial watched Jake close his eyes, waver and then slowly move his left hand in front of him and brought his finger into his chin, his mouth and then his right eye before getting to his nose. Then he moved his right hand in front of his face and fell flat on the ground.

"Enough's enough," Nathanial thought, *"Good enough to take him in."*

Helping the incoherent babbling Jake up, Nathanial helped him to his cruiser, opened the rear door and got him inside. As he was closing the door, Jake looked at him and said, "Did I win the prize, ossifer?"

"You certainly did, Jake," Nathanial replied but even before he had finished, Jake passed out and started falling out the door. *"Lucky those rumbles strips did the job keeping him awake,"* Nathanial thought as he pushed him back in then and went to the truck, got the keys, locked the doors although there wasn't anything worth stealing, and got into his cruiser.

****

Jake was in the jail overnight and then released. His truck had been towed and would be held until he could pick it up. Officer Webster was on patrol and took Jake home. After dropping Jake off in Curran, the opposite direction from where he was headed when Nathanial stopped him, Mitchell reported that Jake thanked the Sheriff profusely for saving his life and possibly the life of others and to tell Nathanial that he certainly had his vote.

Chapter 31

Saturday nights are always busy ones for the members of the Alcona County Sheriff's Department on patrol and the one after the discovery of the body in the cedar copse was no exception for Mitchell Webster. In the early hours of Sunday, he had three D.U.I.s, a brawl at one of the local watering holes and now he was on his way to a "domestic violence" call. A woman had called 911 stating that her husband was irrational and had already hit her. The house—or rather, trailer—was on a dirt road off M-72 about 100 yards from its nearest neighbor.

The night was pitch black with heavy clouds and, consequently, no stars or moonlight. Thus Mitchell parked his cruiser, motor running and the lights on so that he could see his way to the trailer's door and he carried his flashlight. He stepped up on the porch and paused a moment to listen – inside the trailer he could hear yelling, two voices, one female, one male. He knocked on the door and waited. The voices continued so he knocked again and the voices stopped but no one came.

He knocked again.

"Officer Webster, Alcona County Sheriff's Department," he announced.

From inside came a crash, a woman's whimper, and a man's voice, "You bitch. You called the cops."

Mitchell knocked on the door again, "Ma'am, are you alright?"

"Get the fuck away from here, asshole," was the man's response. "We don't need you here."

The woman started to shout something and there was another whack.

"Shut up, bitch, I'll handle this."

"Sir," Mitchell started.

"I said get the fuck away, asshole. You try to come inside and she'll get hurt. Really hurt. Dead hurt."

The incident was escalating swiftly. Mitchell thought, *"Time to call for backup."* He walked back to his car, opened the door and had just seated himself when the trailer's door opened announced by a beam of interior lights brightening the dark outdoors. Mitchell looked up to see a man pointing what seemed to be a rifle at the car. Before he could do anything there was a crack and the muzzle flashed. The cruiser shuddered and the front end on the driver's side dropped.

"I told you to scram, asshole," the man said and Mitchell shoved the gearshift into reverse and scrammed, the front end dragging the ground as he backed around the corner and out of sight behind a copse of scrawny trees, mostly denuded by the winds of fall. He killed the engine and the lights.

"Shots fired," Mitchell screamed into his mike and gave his location. Then he got out of the cruiser carrying his Remington shotgun, went to the trunk, which he unlocked and opened. He grabbed his bulletproof vest and crossed the road behind some scrubs that provided no protection but from which he could see the trailer. Mitchell assumed that the front door was now closed as the only light came though a curtained windowed. He could hear no sounds. He put his vest on, checked his shotgun and his pistol even though he had checked both at the start of the shift and the pistol again before leaving the cruiser.

It was half an hour before his backup arrived and he got out from his cover, turned on his flashlight and waved it down. The cruiser came to a stop in front of him and he was surprised to see it was the Sheriff who was not on duty that night. Nathanial got out of his cruiser wearing his vest and carrying his shotgun and a bullhorn.

"What do you have here, Webster?"

"A man in the trailer armed with a rifle – single shot I think. There is a woman in there. He hit her a couple of times while I was standing at the door – at least that is what it sounded like. Then he told me to scram or he would hurt her so I figured backup was needed."

"You were right," Nathanial agreed.

"When I got into the cruiser to call for backup he came out and shot once. He was lucky or a good shot as he punctured the left front wheel. He may have shot again – I didn't hear one but the engine was roaring as I backed out. He went back in and closed the door. Haven't seen anything or heard anything since then."

"Any cover in front of the house?"

"Not really it ...."

The front door of the cabin burst open and a woman came running out, down the steps and headed for the driveway opening to the road. Mitchell and Nathanial moved across the road toward her. When she was about halfway across the intervening space, the man appeared.2

"You're dead now, bitch," the man screamed, raising his rifle to his shoulder.

The rifle's barrel started tracing her movements and then there was a shot. The rifle stopped its traversing, then fell to the porch and then the man pitched forward off the porch. Nathanial looked at Mitchell who was still in the shooter's pose with his Glock 22 pointed at the house. The woman had stopped her running and had turned to look back at the house.

"Frank," she yelled and started back. Nathanial and Mitchell after her, Mitchell still with his gun ready.

The woman reached the man just moments before Nathanial did. She picked up the rifle, pointed at the man on the ground and pulled the trigger.

"Take that you sonovabitch," she screamed as she tried to rack another shell into the chamber.

Nathanial reached her and coolly took the rifle away from her. Mitchell had put his Glock away and knelt beside the man. Even though the light from the doorway was partially blocked by the porch, he could see a hole in the back of the man's head but he felt his pulse anyway.

"He's dead," Mitchell said. "I'd better call the squad."

He got to his feet and turned toward his cruiser.

"Hold it, Officer Mitchell," Nathanial said holding his hand out. "Give me your weapon."

"What? Why?"

"Officer involved shooting. We'll have to have an investigation. I need your weapon."

"But, he was going to ..."

"Yes, he was and he had shot at you. I don't see a problem but it is not my call. Your weapon please."

Mitchell unholstered his pistol, removed the clip and racked the slide catching the ejected shell and then racked the slide a second time to make certain the weapon was empty. He handed the clip and bullet to Nathanial, who pocketed them, and then the pistol, butt first. Then he walked to his vehicle using his flashlight and stopping to mark the spent cartridge casing to make it easier for the investigating team to find it. In the cruiser he called the squad and reported the shooting to the office just as Rich Jameson pulled his cruiser up behind Nathanial's. Getting out of his vehicle, shotgun at the ready, he asked, "Where's the sheriff."

Mitchell pointed up the driveway and Rich trotted in that direction. Mitchell sat in his cruiser silently for a few minutes, and then he started to shake uncontrollably and tears welled up in his eyes.

***

Three days later Nathanial was testifying at Mitchell's hearing.

"The woman was running directly at us, so any shots fired were at us as well as her and Officer Webster had already been shot at once by this man and quite accurately, I might add. Our investigation has shown that he was a crack shot – rarely missed a deer he shot at. Webster didn't have time to warn him, and truthfully I hadn't reacted fast enough or I might have shot him, too."

Max Reading, presiding hearing officer, asked, "You say Webster fired only the one shot, Sheriff."

"Yes and ballistics confirms this."

"It was dark; the only light was through the doorway so the shooter was just a silhouette?"

"Yes, that's true."

"You're certain that this man, Frank Converse, held a rifle?"

"Yes, I could see the slight gleam of the light on the barrel as he tracked her."

"Just one shot at a silhouetted target?" Max Reading asked again.

"Yes, just one."

"But he hit him smack in the middle of the chest, Sherriff."

"Yes, he did. If you will check his records, you will see that Webster was the top of his class at the range, second in the classroom. At our recent yearly qualifying match, Officer Webster bested everyone by ten points."

"If Webster is such an outstanding officer, why did he come here, heartland of the boonies of Up North?"

"He is from the area, grew up in Au Gres and wanted to be home."

"I guess we can be glad that he did."

"I certainly am," Nathanial confided. "I might be dead if he hadn't."

The hearing board didn't take long to make their decision and Officer Mitchell Webster was back on duty the following day.

Chapter 32

"Thank you, Dave, for that update," Ed Stockwell said. "It has reach the point in the meeting to pause for refreshments featuring ..." and he looked at George Jameson who was the host for the meeting.

"Killer Double Fudge Walnut Brownies," George said. "Gert said she never made these before so she won't attest to their goodness."

"Can't be much goodness in something named like that but there certainly has to be some good taste."

He slammed the gavel on the table.

"Ten – make that fifteen – minute recess."

Wednesday night, the last Sportsman meeting of the year, held this night in the party/meeting room of the west side fire department. Meetings alternated between the west side and the east side. One of the board members was always selected to provide the goodies and those always came from Gert, complete with a big pot of coffee. Break time was usually the highlight of the meeting.

Dugal made his way to the table where coffee and brownies awaited finding the goody plate to be half empty he judged. Myrna was just leaving with a brownie in each hand.

"One's for John," she exclaimed guiltily, "but if they're half as good as they sound, he'll have to come get his own."

"I'll try to leave a few," Dugal said.

His way to the plate apparently free, he was reaching for one of the smaller ones, when a voice from behind him declared, "You can't have seconds when some of us haven't had firsts."

He turned to see George Jameson grinning broadly.

"I would think that you being the provider of these delectable sounding things, you are probably here for thirds."

"Ah, Dugal. You caught me again," and then sotto voce, "it's actually fourths but don't tell anyone."

He nudged Dugal aside and grabbed two, giving one to Dugal.

"Step aside with me, I'd like a word with you."

Dugal followed George out of the crowd until they were standing by themselves.

"You've been pretty involved this summer," George noted. "How come you didn't run for the board in August?"

"I'm not a leader. More of a follower and worker, like you."

"Wish that was true," George said. "I had to fight them off again this year, wanting me to take Stockwell's place. I told 'em that he'd only been president for three years and was just learning how to do things."

"Well, if you're just a worker, why are you on the board?"

"Someone has to. It doesn't take much anyway. Just coordinating a couple of things like the road cleanup and getting stuff for these meetings. That's easy. I just call Gert."

"Well, maybe in three or four years," Dugal said unconvincingly, "after I've learned my way around the group. Remember I just moved here in March."

"Heck of time to move in, there was still snow on the ground."

"True," Dugal agreed, "but it gave us time to get unpacked and the inside shipshape before moving to the outside. Then everything else started keeping us busy."

"Like?" George asked.

"This organization and Hic-Cup."

"You do that? I used to but, honestly, staying up that late knocked me out for two days. I'm just not a night owl."

"I got used to late nights driving trucks and Earleen, that's my wife, stayed up waiting for me on those nights I got in late – and there were many of them."

"Well, keep it in mind. Say, let me ask you something else while I've got you alone."

Now the real reason you wanted to talk to me, Dugal thought as he took a bite. "Man," he said as chocolate goodness titillated his taste buds, "These are to die for."

George nodded his agreement and launched into his question.

"What do you think of this Jefferson? I know you were high school teammates, word gets around, and you're a little buddy-buddy so you can knock off the friends stuff."

"You mean, do I think he can do the job as sheriff?"

"Yeah, that's it."

"I thought this organization was politically neutral."

"Yes," George said as he put the last half of his brownie in his mouth and glanced longingly at the table trying to see if there were more, "but that's in the meeting proper – we don't let candidates talk, etc. But as long as it's not in the meeting."

"He knows the job and I think runs a good department, much more than that I can't say," Dugal confided.

"Well, he hasn't found anything about girl you found and then this other one. Nothing coming out about that."

"It takes a while to get id and DNA when you have a partially decomposed body, or that's what I hear. I think he told the press everything he could."

"They say we have a serial killer on our hands. My wife's a little nervous with the grandkids coming up for Thanksgiving."

"The murders – retract that, I don't know if they are – the deaths are ten years apart. That usually doesn't mean a serial killer …"

"But there could be other bodies, you know, hidden as well as the first one."

"Maybe we are drop-off spot," Jim Winchell chimed in joining the group, "You know, the girls don't seem to be from around here …"

"How do you know this second one was a girl?" Jerry asked, joining the group. "Nothing's been said."

"Well, if it's a serial killer, it would be wouldn't it," Jim retorted.

"Could be a woman or maybe a boy," Dugal said.

Then to George, "You asked me if I thought Nathanial could do the job. Yes, he can but making statements like, 'We have a serial killer on the loose', won't help and all it will do is to get people more worried than they are. I think we should wait for the law enforcement people to do their job. They'll let us know when they know something. I think it's the law."

At that opportune moment, Ed Stockwell slammed the gavel, "Get your coffee and take a seat. Let's get this meeting over with."

The four headed back to their respective seats, George gazing longingly at a now empty brownie plate as Dugal managed to snatch the last one.

Chapter 33

For Nathanial, things remained that way for the next couple of days. After getting no answer at the Duncan residence, Nathanial had called the Huntington Woods police department and they had sent a car. No one was home and a neighborhood canvas revealed that they had gone away for two weeks but no one knew where. Neighbors had been asked to watch the house while they were gone, one of them had a key if needed but of course it wasn't. Not even their employers knew where they were.

It was Sunday afternoon, four days after Jennifer Duncan's body was discovered that Nathanial's office forwarded a phone call from Peter Miller.

"Sheriff Jefferson," Peter began. "My wife said you needed to talk to me."

"Yes, Mr. Miller," Nathanial gazed longingly at the plate of ham, peas, scalloped potatoes and cornbread that he had just fixed for himself. He looked at Dawn and shrugged.

"In early May, you pulled a vehicle back on to the road at the Hibbard Pond Path S-curve.

Peter was silent for a minute.

"Is there something wrong with that?"

"No, not at all. Did you?"

"Yes, I did."

"Whose was it?"

"Don't rightly remember. I got a call and went and pulled it up and was paid in cash. Hell of a lot of work, too."

"Your wife intimated to my deputy that you knew the person and, just to make our position clear, Mr. Miller, this is part of a mysterious death investigation and not answering my questions makes you a party to that."

Again there was silence on the other end of the phone, and then Peter mumbled something.

"Speak up, Mr. Miller," Nathanial said, "I didn't understand you."

"Nick Williston."

"How do you know him?"

"We went to high school together and went through boot camp together. That's how we became friends. Hadn't heard from him in years but knew that he lived somewhere over at Hibbard Pond. His folks had a place. He had told me about it during boot camp. We would talk when the lights went out, he had the upper ..."

"*Ancient history*," Nathanial thought.

"Yes, Mr. Miller. Tell me about the recovery."

"His truck had lost a wheel. He said he had a flat during that freak snowstorm and he didn't have the spare on properly. He skidded trying to avoid something in the road and went over the edge. Guess he was knocked out or something. When he got himself out, he said he had walked home, said it was several miles, called me and then walked back to meet me. He was there by the time I was."

"Was there anyone else?"

"No, just him. He was really handy helping me get that old pickup of his up the hill. Course the snow made it easier. By time I got there he had it dug out, must have had a shovel in the truck or brought one from home and the snow was starting to melt."

"Right," Nathanial interjected. "Where did you take the truck?"

"Bob Wright's place. It's a small auto repair shop over toward Ossineke."

"I know where it is. Thank you, Mr. Miller. I'll need you to come into our office in Harrisville at your earliest convenience and make a statement."

"Yes, sir, I will."

"That's tomorrow or Tuesday at the latest."

"Yes, sir, tomorrow for sure."

"And one other thing, Mr. Miller," Nathanial said sternly.

"Yes, sir."

"As I said, this is an ongoing investigation. Although we don't know if Nick Williston has done anything wrong, if we find out that he did and that you warned him about this investigation, I will charge you as an accessory."

He heard Miller gulp.

"No, sir, I won't say a thing."

"Good idea, Mr. Miller. Because if Williston is involved and you warn him, you will face the same penalty as he does. And although we don't have a death penalty in Michigan, that means life imprisonment."

Miller was silent and then answered meekly, "Yes, sir. I'll be over to your office in the morning. Anything else, sheriff?"

"No, that's it, Mr. Miller. See you tomorrow."

Putting the phone down, Nathanial turned his attention to his slowly cooling dinner.

*****

First thing Monday morning, Mitchell Webster visited Wright's Auto Repair 'We Make It Wright' and learned nothing to aid in the investigation. The truck had been brought in and he had fixed the rear wheel and sold Williston a new set of tires; well, not new, Bob Wright said, retreads because Weird Willie wouldn't spring for new.

"Weird Willie," Mitchell had said.

"Yeah," Wright smiled, "He is really a strange coot. Don't see him very often. Guess he does most of the work on that old truck himself but folks around here who know him, and there aren't many, have hung that nickname on him. It fits, too."

Mitchell obtained a copy of the bill, marked "Cash" and admonished Bob Wright not to say anything.

*****

True to his word, Peter Miller showed up at the Harrisville office driving his wrecker early the next morning. Nathanial met with him and recorded his statement that varied little from what he had said the previous night. Nathanial already knew that Bob Wright had nothing to offer so he took the opportunity to question Miller further. Miller said there was nothing to add and then Nathanial took him through the recovery step by step.

"When I got there I could see the truck and Williston down there with a shovel. I shouted at him and he waved and then scrambled up the hill. He was a lot better doing that in the slush and snow than I would have been. He always was a better athlete – one of the best in our platoon.

"I turned the truck around, put flares and cones to warn any traffic – although there wasn't any. I set the stability pads and fed out the cable. Nick took it down the hill and attached it under the rear of the truck. He knew what he was doing so I let him. I sure as hell didn't want to go down that hill and then have to get back up.

"Then we pulled it up the hill. Took almost half an hour."

"Anything else?"

"Nope ..." Peter paused. "Wait, we started pulling up, Nick was down there in case something went wrong, and the truck started to slew, 'cause the front wheels were turned. He got in the truck and set them straight. Tied the steering wheel with a rope he jammed with the door. Then, just after he gave me the okay sign, he waved for me to stop. He reached through the door and got something. Wound up and heaved it into the woods. Then we pulled the truck up."

Nathanial jumped on that.

"What was it?"

"What was what?"

"The thing he threw?"

"Don't know. Just a rag or something. But it must have been heavy because he threw it high and it went far, probably crotched up in one of them trees."

"Thanks ..." Nathanial started to get up.

"Red."

"What?"

"Red. It was red, whatever he threw was red."

"Thanks, Mr. Miller. Now you just wait while this is typed so you can sign it and ..."

"Yes," Peter answered hopefully.

"Remember to keep this to yourself."

Peter's shoulders slumped in defeat.

"Yes, sir."

Chapter 34

Thirty minutes later, Nathanial was at the S-curve meeting Mitchell Webster and his two forensic men Bob Roberts and Rich Walker. The four clambered down the slope.

"The truck should have been about right here from what Miller said," explained Nathanial. "So the driver's door is here and he threw something up in the air toward the woods so we'll need to look high. Don't think we did that before when we found the body."

"Wasn't any need," Walker said.

"Well, now there is."

"What are we looking for?" Bob Roberts asked.

"A Tickle Me Elmo."

"A what?" Mitchell exclaimed.

"A red doll. Something red. Now let's get at it."

Nathanial indicated search areas and they started looking. It was slow going especially in the cedar copses. It was two hours before Rich Walker shouted.

"Over here. It's up in one of these cedars."

The four gathered and gazed upwards where a ball of red was barely visible through the thick foliage of the cedar.

"It's crotched against the trunk by two limbs. No way we can shake it done. We'll need a ladder," Rich said as the four stood contemplating the situation.

"Not a problem," Nathanial said pulling out his cell phone, "if we have service."

And they did. Within a minute Nathanial was connected.

"Chet, Sheriff Jefferson here. I need a 30 or 40 foot ladder at the bottom of the S-curve on the north side."

Chet Johnson, fire chief of the east side fire department, replied.

"Call it a kitten rescue," Nathanial said. "You'll see our cars parked at the south end of the turn. And, time is of the essence."

Nathanial realized that if Peter Miller was good enough friends with Nick Williston, he might contact him, and if Williston was guilty he would run. "*Or at least I would,*" Nathanial thought.

Being a volunteer group it took half an hour before they heard a loud motor approaching from the north, pass, and brake to a stop. Then there was excited jabbering, clanging, silence for a minute and then the jabbering resumed. Soon it became understandable.

"Would you two just cooperate. Geez, why did you have to be handy for this one."

Bob Roberts looked at Nathanial and shrugged.

"Tater and the Dum Dees."

They were well known to many in the county, especially law enforcement but not that they were the criminal type, just that their antics caused trouble sometimes.

Within a minute, the three became visible carrying a long multi-sectional aluminum ladder, Tater in the lead, Second in the middle (being the shortest) and First on the other end. First's end was higher than Tater and Nathanial doubted that the short Second was doing much to help.

"Greetings, Sheriff," Tater said bringing the ladder company to a halt.

"Top of the ..." Second said.

"Morning," finished First.

"Which tree is the kitten in?" Tater asked.

"Why so many cops?" First queried.

"Must be a kitten litter," Second answered and chortled.

"Enough," Nathanial said and the DumDees quieted.

"That tree," Nathanial indicated, "near the top."

The three, with the requisite nattering and slapstick, extended the ladder with some effort, wedged the bottom firmly in the ground and then Second started up, First and Tater holding the bottom.

"Hold on," Nathanial said and Second did. "We'll take it from here."

"But I'm good with cats," Second said. "I's got four."

"It's not a cat. It's evidence."

Second quickly slid down the few rungs he had climbed.

"Okay," Nathanial said to his forensic duo, "who gets the honors?"

Bob and Rich looked at each other "Coin toss," they said simultaneously.

"My turn," Rich said. "On three. One, two, ..." and he flipped an imaginary coin into the air as Bob shouted, "Tails."

Catching the coin and slapping it onto the back of his hand, Rich looked and said, "Tails, it is."

Bob immediately started up the ladder, camera at the ready.

"What the ...," First said and Second finished "...hell?"

Rich laughed.

"We always used to toss coins for onerous jobs when we were together. Then one day neither of us had a coin. So Bob came up with the idea. The moment the 'coin' is tossed by one of us, both of us think heads or tails but the non-tosser yells his choice. Then when the 'coin' is revealed the tosser says his."

"Is that fair?" Tater asked.

"Well," Rich mused, "so far it's 47 for Bob, 45 for me. I'd say that's fair."

"I'm here," Bob shouted the top of the ladder, firmly held by First and Tater.

Nathanial had followed Bob's progress up the ladder and asked, "What can you see?"

Bob paused in his documenting picture taking.

"Red, a little yellow, and a beady eye."

"Just one?"

"That's all for now. Hold the ladder, I'm going to get it."

After pulling on a latex glove, Bob reached into the tree, stretching.

"Got it," as the Tickle Me Elmo appeared in his gloved hand.

Nathanial could see there was only one eye.

"Which eye is gone?"

"Left one," Bob answered as him backed down the ladder clutching Elmo in his right hand.

"That's Jennifer's," Nathanial said. "At least the description said the left eye was missing but it's been five years. Ought to satisfy Jed Parker though."

Reaching the bottom of the ladder, Elmo was deposited into an evidence bag held by Rich Walker. Duly identified by Walker, the bag was handed to Nathanial.

"I'm off to get a warrant," Nathanial said. "You two are done for now," to the forensics team, "but stand by. Mitchell, you be certain they get the truck out of here and then meet me at the office."

On the way to his cruiser followed by Rich and Bob, Nathanial could hear the requisite chatter of Dum Dees with Tater giving directions and then the clang clatter of the ladder settling into its collapsed posture. Nathanial shook his head and muttered, "More like the Three Stooges."

*****

"Run this by me again," Jed Parker, Alcona County Prosecutor, asked Nathanial. "You want a search warrant as well as an arrest warrant for kidnapping and harmful endangerment for Nicholas Williston?"

Parker was sitting behind his desk in Harrisville half an hour later.

"We found a body in the woods north of the S-curve last week. It had been there for some time and has been identified as that of Jennifer Duncan who was snatched from a parking lot in the Detroit area five years ago. She was three and a half at the time, which makes her eight and a half or so at the time of her death about four months ago. Her parents have not been notified so there has been no public announcement of her name. Also, until today we have not had any idea how she got there.

"Peter Miller runs a towing operation out of Posen and the morning after that freak snowstorm in early May he had a call from Nick Williston, known around as Weird Willie we found out. Williston's pickup had gone off the S-curve during the storm and he wanted Miller to pull him out. Miller did and was paid in cash by Williston and asked not to report it so he didn't. During the recovery, actually just before they started pulling the truck up the hill, Miller saw Williston throw something from the seat of the pickup into the woods. This morning we searched and found a Tickle Me Elmo doll crotched in a cedar.

The doll was missing its left eye. Jennifer's favorite toy was a Tickle Me Elmo and it was missing its left eye. It was also missing from the car where Jennifer was last seen."

"So you think that Jennifer was in the truck when it went over the side and she died and Williston buried her in the woods before calling Miller?" Parker had put his feet up on his desk and was holding his hands in a prayerful attitude under his chin.

"Yes. How she died we don't know but it wasn't by violence and we do know that she had the flu. Could be that Williston was trying to get her to a doctor, not much other reason for him to be out with her during the storm."

"Mighty slim tie there, Nathanial."

"I know but ... and this will seem strange ... one of the reported sightings of Jennifer during the AMBER Alert was in Standish."

"Still ..."

"Yes, and there is possibly a tie in with the girl in the perch pond. She isn't, doesn't appear to be, from around here either. She was young, buried secretly, discovered by accident. We might be able to get something from the Elmo to tie it in better but probably not as it's been in the weather for four months."

"What do you know about Williston?"

"He's a loner. Grew up here, went to school here, joined the army after graduation, went to Nam for one tour, got out, came back here. Parents died in a house fire. He lives on 200 acres near Hibbard Pond. A loner, no one recalls seeing him with Jennifer or anyone for that matter."

Nathanial was silent for a moment.

"My concern is that if he is guilty, he'll run. The longer we wait the more likely it is that Miller will contact him. Williston has no phone or no phone that we know of. He may have a throwaway cell phone. Miller doesn't have a number so he can't call but he could stop by."

"It's a long shot, Nathanial."

"Yes, I know, Jed. We did find some smudged and partial fingerprints on the tarp. They are not a certain match for Williston but they could be his."

"Again that isn't proof enough. Circumstantial at best but possibly could be used in court."

"I agree, but they were both young. Both probably abducted. True, I don't know about the perch pond girl but she died a violent death and was buried secretly. She deserves better – they both do."

"I agree. Magistrate Judy is doing warrants. It may make a difference that she lost a kid at an early age. All I can do is give it a shot."

"Thanks. I'll be in my office. Already have my team in place."

Chapter 35

He swung the axe, splitting the piece of oak cleanly. Bending over he picked up one of the pieces to throw it on the pile of freshly split wood, today he should finish splitting the last of his winter's supply. Then he stopped abruptly in mid-swing, the heavy piece of wood tearing from his grasp and falling halfway to the pile he had started barely an hour before.

Something was wrong.

Fearful, he glanced up at the cabin porch. Sue Ellen was there playing with her dolls just as she had been when he looked five minutes before. Not her – then what? His senses were atingle – something was wrong. Swinging the axe, he embedded it in the stump he used as the splitting block. He turned, stripping off his gloves as he did so, dropping them heedlessly to the ground and simultaneously picking up his shotgun from where it leaned again the fender of his truck.

Breaking the old double barrel bird-hunting shotgun from his youth, he walked quickly ten steps toward the cabin. Making certain, for the fourth time that day, that it was loaded, he snapped it shut, and stopped. Turning slowing around counter-clockwise and sweeping the shotgun like a backward running second hand of a watch, his eyes seemed to see everything. A complete circuit and nothing was out of place. At least nothing that he could see but something was wrong. He knew it. He sensed it. Just as he knew that something was wrong that night in Nam when the Cong had almost overrun his base. He had been the one who had shouted the warning only seconds before the first salvo.

Five more steps and another sweep, this one clockwise, just in case he caught someone expecting him to do as before. But there was nothing. He looked to the sky. Cloudless as it had been all day but ... then he heard it. Had there been the normal sounds of the woods, he might not have but for some reason, he now sensed, the woods were quiet. Motors, more than one – that meant cars coming up his road. He was being invaded. Whoever it was had gotten his gate open and was coming up the road, moving fast he knew because otherwise he might not have heard the sound. His plan never had been to stand and fight – it had always been to run. That was one of the lessons he learned in Nam, if you're outnumbered and out-gunned – run. Whoever was coming would have the advantage both in numbers and guns. His only advantage was in knowledge of the terrain. So he would run – Sue Ellen's safety was paramount.

"Sue Ellen, get your coat and bag. Hurry." Three steps and he leapt upon to the porch. "Now, move it, girl."

Sue Ellen looked up at him, her face evidencing her fear at the call.

"Fast ... licketty split," he said as he entered the cabin throwing the door back, slamming it against the wall. He grabbed his hunting rifle, and the ammunition bag, both hanging from the antler rack by the door. Two strides took him across the room where two knapsacks sat on a log chair. He leaned the shotgun against the chair and picked up the larger of the knapsacks only after he had put the loop of the ammo bag over his head and thrust his free arm through it. Then the strap of the largest knapsack went on one shoulder. He picked up the other knapsack using the hand with the deer rifle, and grabbed the shotgun with the other hand, all this as he was whirling to face the door and he was moving again.

Back on the porch Sue Ellen was just getting up. He didn't say a word, propped the shotgun against the rail, picked her up and grasped her securely with the other arm, crotching her in his elbow. He picked up the shotgun and headed for the truck, Sue Ellen kicking and screaming that she had forgotten her Reggie. Ten quick running strides and he reached the truck, shotgun against the truck bed, door open, Sue Ellen thrust inside screaming, knapsacks and ammo bag into the bed, rifle and shotgun into the gun rack behind the driver's seat. He was behind the wheel before Sue Ellen had quit bouncing. He fastened her quickly in her booster seat, clicking the seat belt securely. By then she had stopped her screaming because she sensed something was wrong. The truck was moving before she could say anything.

He swung the truck around and threw it into first gear, gunning the engine that roared to life leaping forward as he shifted effortlessly into second and then third. The truck blew past the cabin, heading for a dim opening in the trees on the small side of the clearing. There was no braking, he knew he needed all the speed he could manage if they were as close as he thought they were.

And they were. Barely had the rear of his truck disappeared into the gloomy darkness of the woods then Nathanial's SUV entered the clearing, red and blue lights blazing because there was no longer any need for secrecy and, as he had told his deputies, "With your lights on, we'll know you're not Williston."

As he rounded the front of the cabin, he braked to a stop, rear end skidding so that his vehicle ended up pointed at the cabin. Immediately he sensed something was wrong because the cabin door stood wide open. He was out of his vehicle, gun drawn whirling around looking for any sign of life. There were none, except for a faint trail of dust settling to the ground in front of a dark spot in the trees to his right. Into his vehicle again, and heading for the opening, he keyed his mike, "Mitchell, secure the cabin. Ralph, follow me."

The road through the woods was rutty and small trees were growing up in places as it had been over a year since he had used this road. It ran through his woods and ended up on a dirt road running through Big Stag Club Property. From there was just half a mile to Hibbard Pond Path, five miles from his gate. If the authorities didn't know about this road, he'd be safe, at least for a while. He had found the old road from the Big Stag Club Property running about half a mile into his folk's place as a kid. When he was building his log cabin, he used some of the trees cut to make this road as an escape route but at the time he didn't know from what he might be escaping. Fire had been a thought but that wouldn't explain the S-curve he had built into it. That was to slow down anyone who didn't know the road.

Gunning the engine for the straight dash after coming out of the last turn of the S-curve, he chanced a glance at Sue Ellen. Her eyes were wide and her face as white as a ghost. It was that glance that did him in. As his eyes came back to the road, a dark bulk seemed to rise up in front of him. He slammed on the breaks and turned the wheel to the right. What stopped him was not his brakes but a huge red oak that had been growing there for over 100 years. The force of the truck hitting that oak threw both him and Sue Ellen forward. Only his buckling her in saved her from careening forward into the truck's dashboard or window.

He wasn't as fortunate as he had not buckled himself in and his chest slammed into the steering wheel which was coming back to meet him. His door flew open and he was ejected from the truck, falling lifelessly to the ground in the middle of the road.

Twenty feet away the giant stag watched the entire thing from where he had stopped after stepping out of the trees in front of the truck. He didn't move for several seconds until he saw the flashing red and blue lights through the trees and heard the roar of Nathanial's engine. Then he moved slowly into the woods, pausing ten feet from the road to look back at the scene. Watching events unfold for a minute, he snorted almost with finality and slowly walked deeper into his domain.

Nathanial's SUV skidded to a stop just feet from where Williston's body lay. He keyed his mike, "Get that squad up here and down this road. We have at least one in need."

Quickly he got to the door of the truck and looked in. Sue Ellen seemed lifeless, eyes closed, and Nathanial's heart sank. Then her hand twitched and he breathed again. He knew better than to touch her – the squad would be here in minutes. He walked to where Williston lay, sprawled on his back, seemingly sightless eyes looking skyward, the trauma to his chest clearly evident. Nathanial knelt beside him and grasped a wrist to check his pulse. He heard Williston breathe, a gasping inhalation of air and then a coughing wheeze as blood bubbled from the gaping chest. Nathanial looked at Williston's face and found himself looking into his black eyes. His lips moved and Nathanial leaned closer.

"Sue Ellen?" Williston asked. "Is she …"

"She's fine," Nathanial said uncertain if he was correct.

"Good," wheezed Williston, "she …"

There was a deep sigh and rattle as the air exited from his chest and his gleaming black eyes went dim.

A sound startled Nathanial and he looked into the woods and saw movement.

"Hey," he said and then stopped, as he knew his words would only be heard by uncomprehending ears.

Chapter 36

Ralph's cruiser came around the corner and braked to a stop and Nathanial started toward it hand in the air. Ralph stuck his head out.

"Get your cruiser back so the squad can get in here closer. Hitch a ride with them. See me when you get back."

Ralph waved to acknowledge his understanding and started backing his cruiser out. Nathanial returned to his cruiser and keyed his mike.

"Mitchell, report in."

"Yes, sir. There is no one in the cabin."

"You didn't disturb anything, did you?"

"No, sir. Walked into every room. Looked in every closet."

"Did you ..."

"Yes, sir. I had on gloves."

"Okay, stay there. Our forensics team is on the way. They'll secure the place. Butch?"

"Yes, sir."

"Stay at the gate. No reporters of any kind. Make certain no one sneaks in with the official cars. Our forensics team should be on the way. As soon as we have a way in we'll call for a tow truck. The squad will probably be coming out with the girl. There will probably be another squad to get Williston. I'm sure he is a goner."

"Roger."

"Sheriff out."

Putting the mike back, Nathanial went to where Williston lay. Kneeling, he once again felt for a pulse. From his right breast pocket he took a plastic sheath and pulled out a shinny piece of metal. He held this in front of Williston's mouth and nose but nothing happened. He looked at Williston's chest. There was no movement, no flow of blood. He sighed. He had wanted him alive. There were so many questions to answer and now ... maybe there would be no answers.

A small sound startle him and he stood up and hurried to the door of the truck. Looking in he saw the girl looking back at him, green eyes wide.

"Hi," Nathanial said. "Are you alright?"

That started the flow of tears but she held her arms out to him. He leaned into the truck, released her seatbelt and took her into his arms. He got out of the truck and started walking back the way he had come. Once in his arms she had quieted.

Nathanial looked down at her and she looked back.

"You're going to be alright, Sue Ellen," he said, remembering what Williston had called her.

She stared back at him for a moment thinking.

"Yes, Lynn is alright. Not Sue Ellen. I'm Lynn."

Nathanial smiled at her, searching his memory and having it click in. If he was right, a couple in Sylvania, Ohio, would be glad to get the news that their daughter was alive and well.

Red and white lights flashing, the squad came around the corner. Ralph was the first one out followed by Second and a moment later by First, exiting the driver's side.

"Not you two," Nathanial said, "I want competent aid, not a couple of Dum Dees."

"Don't worry," First said, "We know what we're doing and we don't fool around on this job."

"Besides," Second chimed in, "Tater's not here and we mostly do it to annoy him."

They looked at each other, nodded and then First reached for Lynn.

"I think she's alright," Nathanial said as he handed Lynn to First. "She was buckled in and the truck struck the tree by the left front. Williston," he said gesturing toward the body "is over there. I'm certain that he is dead."

By this time two more first responders had come out of the back of the squad and hurried to help.

"Ralph," Nathanial said. "You look like you need some exercise. Take a walk down this road and find out where it goes. When you find a main road or known access to the main road let Butch know. He'll call a tow truck, which will probably need to come in that way to get Williston's truck. When you come back, bring my cruiser. Keys are in it."

Ralph set out immediately first walking until he cleared the truck and Williston's body and then at a trot. Nathanial turned and headed for the cabin, pausing as he came to the back of the squad where the four first responders were attending to Lynn Dewey.

"You were right, sheriff, he's a goner. Should have buckled up," First said as he got a blanket and headed to cover the corpse.

Nathanial sighed.

"Even the dead, no matter how heinous they have been, deserved some respect," he thought.

"How's she doing?" he asked the three working over Lynn.

"Fine, sheriff, as far as we can tell. We get her to Alpena General for a thorough examination though."

"Good, can I get a picture?"

Nathanial had taken out his cell phone.

"Yes, sir," Second said and the three moved out of the picture's frame.

"Smile, Lynn," Nathanial said, "This is for mommy and daddy."

She smiled brightly and Nathanial took her picture. He would call the Deweys as soon as he had a signal. A five-minute walk brought him back to the clearing. In addition to Mitchell's cruiser, there were two others, lights off, parked in front of the cabin. Mitchell's cruiser still had its lights on.

"Mitchell," Nathanial said striding toward the cabin.

"Yes, sir," Mitchell answered from his right.

Nathanial stopped and stood still watching as Mitchell jogged toward him.

"Why aren't you at the cabin?"

"The techs told me they had everything under control. So I decided to have a look around. There's a garden behind the cabin, still has some corn stalks and pumpkins. Looks like red skinned potatoes too. Some of them had been dug up. And," Mitchell continued, pointing over his shoulder, "there are two graves over there."

"Graves?"

"Yes, sir, two graves. One with a big cross and one with a little one."

Nathanial mused, "That might explain ... We'll have to exhume the bodies and try to get some id. Good job, Mitchell. Now go turn the lights on your cruiser off."

Nathanial continued on to the cabin pulling out his cell phone to check for service. It was weak but he had a signal. But, first things first. He put on a pair of latex gloves, just in case and stepped inside. Bob Roberts was working in the great room, if that is what it was, dusting for prints on a cabinet that stood against the far wall.

"Excuse me, Bob" Nathanial said.

Roberts stopped and turned to face him, "Yes, Sheriff."

Rich came in from the other room.

"We got a dead man about half a mile down the south road through the woods. It's going to be dark soon so I would appreciate it if you could get your work done with him quickly. Then we could get the body moved before dark and not have to worry about a guard."

"Certainly, the work here isn't going anywhere," Rich said.

"Coin toss," he said to Bob.

Nathanial heard a vehicle and turned to see the squad stop outside the door and left without waiting for an answer.

First was leaning out of the window.

"We left Fred with the body."

"Thanks. Taking her to Alpena General?"

"Yep, she's fine. Fell asleep."

"Check her in as Baby Doe. Don't mention any other names. Got it?"

"Got it."

"Fred can catch a ride with us or the next unit that comes for the body."

"Hell, he's a volunteer too and can use the supplement."

First waved and the squad drove off, lights flashing more for effect than need at this point.

Mitchell was standing by his cruiser.

"Go down to the crash site with Bob or Rich whoever wins or loses the coin toss. I don't know how they're working this one. Send the first responder back here and stay there until the body and truck are removed. You can get a ride with the last of them."

"Yes, sir," Mitchell said.

Nathanial returned to the great room meeting Roberts on his way out.

"You win or lose?" Nathanial asked.

"Depends on how you look at it," Roberts smiled as he said it.

"There is also the victim's truck that needs to be gone over. Probably be best if it were towed to our garage."

"I agree. Won't take long to do the body, I expect."

"No," agreed Nathanial. "Of course, we'll need his prints. Mitchell is outside if he could get a ride with you, he'll take over for the first responder who is there."

With that settled, Nathanial went out to the porch and pulled out his cell phone and called his office.

"Barbara Ann, we've secured the place. Williston is dead, ran and hit a tree with his truck. There was a young girl with him. No one else here. I am going to send you a picture. Go on line to the National Center site and compare it to the picture of Lynn Dewey, the girl who was snatched three months ago in Sylvania, Ohio. If it's a match, get the parents home phone number and give me a call."

He sent the picture and waited, watching Robert's squad with he and Mitchell pass on the way to the woods.

Three minutes later, his phone rang.

"It's her, sheriff," and she gave him the Deweys' number.

Jim Dewey answered the phone.

"Mr. Dewey, this is Sheriff Nathanial Jefferson of Alcona County, Michigan."

"Yes," Dewey answered apprehensively.

"Sir, I don't want to alarm you but I would like to send a picture to a cell phone or computer of a young girl we believe might be your daughter."

A gasp came from the phone.

"She's not the one ..."

"No, sir. This little girl is fine, sir. She's been in an automobile accident and is on her way to Alpena General Hospital for further examination."

"Thank God," Dewey breathed.

"Sir, I believe she is your daughter but do need your id. She says her name is Lynn."

He heard Dewey talking to his wife, "It's her, they found her, she's okay."

Then to Nathanial, he gave his cell phone number.

"I'll send the picture as soon as we hang up. Please call me back when you have identified the girl."

It took less than a minute after the picture had been sent for Nathanial's phone to ring. He saw it was Dewey.

"That's her" was the first thing he heard.

Then they discussed how to get to Alpena. Dewey declined a police escort Nathanial offered. Nathanial put his cell phone away, a broad smile on his face. Then he remembered and called the tip line for the National Center for Missing and Exploited Children to report a potential successful recovery.

It was a long night for Mitchell in the woods, as the body wasn't removed for two hours and the truck for five. The body removal hadn't been easy because the Hibbard Pond Funeral Home couldn't make it beyond the start of the S-Curve so Wallace and the assistant he brought had to carry it by litter to the hearse. Then his ride was the tow truck that first had gone down the road from the clearing and pulled the truck free from the tree. Then it had gone down Williston's access road to the Path, south to the road leading into Big Stag property and backing up Williston's escape road to the truck. The tow truck dropped him off at the entrance to Williston's property where Butch still stood guard from the comfort of his cruiser. From there Mitchell had to walk to the cabin and his cruiser in the dark as he had forgotten his flashlight and Butch refused to part with his. By that time the forensic team was done with its initial job and had left. Nathanial was waiting for him.

"Good job, Mitchell. Stay here until Carmody comes in a couple of hours. Then you're off until 8:00."

"8:00," stammered Mitchell.

"Yes," replied Nathanial as he headed for his car and a few hours in his bed before what he knew would be a hectic couple of days. "That's when your shift starts, doesn't it?"

Chapter 37

It was a short night for Nathanial as well as Jim Dewey contacted him to say that he had called a Press Conference at Alpena General for 8:00 a.m. Nathanial arrive at the hospital at 7:30 and had a brief chat with the Deweys.

Precisely at 8:00, the Deweys entered a small auditorium provided by the hospital. Nathanial was surprised at the crowd. There were eighteen people there including a man and woman handling the camera for Channel 11.

Dewey stepped to the microphone.

"Thank you all for coming," he said. "I called this conference to tell you that our daughter Lynn was found alive yesterday by the Alcona County sheriff's department headed by Sheriff Nathanial Jefferson."

The room erupted in applause. There were shouts of "Mr. Dewey" and "Sheriff Jefferson," but Jim help up his hand and the room quieted.

"Sheriff Jefferson has asked me not to say anything except about Lynn and," he nodded at Nathanial "truth be told, I don't know much. The sheriff has been pretty close-mouthed about everything but has promised to say a few words and accept questions after my brief statement."

"The sheriff found Lynn in a pickup truck that had run into a tree. She was belted in a booster seat and other than some bruising is fine. She is healthy, by that I mean not undernourished, and shows no signs of ill treatment. The doctor is going to look at her in an hour and then we should be permitted to take her home. I am asking you to please respect our privacy, do not attempt to take pictures or follow us. If you do, the sheriff has promised me that both he and the highway patrol will not take kindly to this. In a few days, once Lynn is secure in her home and the household is back to normal, we will hold another press conference in Sylvania. Until then phone calls will be forwarded to an answering machine and the Sylvania police have guaranteed us that our home will be our castle.

"Now I am willing to answer a few questions."

A woman in the second row stood up immediately and asked, "Mr. Dewey, are you sorry you quit the race for the U.S. House of Representatives?"

Jim was obviously shocked by the question and for a moment seemed disoriented. Then he seemed to gather himself and asked her what paper she worked for. She told him.

"Well, if my name carries any weight at all with the editor of your paper, and if he is the kind of person I think an editor should be, you won't be working there tomorrow."

To the rest of the people he said, "I'm sorry. I am no longer in the mood for questions."

Jim Dewey nodded to Nathanial, took his wife's arm, and the two of them walked out as other reporters shouted questions at them. The young lady in the second row seemed not to believe what was going on.

Nathanial stepped to the microphone.

"The investigation that led to Lynn Dewey's return is an ongoing investigation and therefore, I am not going to say very much about it. When I feel that I can tell you more, I will be happy to do so. For now, we are glad the Lynn is unharmed and with her parents.

"I will accept a few questions but, like Mr. Dewey," and he looked straight at the young lady in the second row, "if I deem them callous or inappropriate, I will not answer them."

In the second row the young lady in question simply mouthed "Callous or inappropriate?"

Hands were in the air; shouts of "Sheriff" and "Sheriff Jefferson" were heard. Nathanial indicated a middle-aged man in the third row.

"Does this any investigation have anything to do with the body in the perch pond?"

"As of now, we are uncertain."

From a middle-aged woman in the first row, "Does it involve the body found last week in the woods of the Great Stag Club?"

Though he had known this would be asked, he didn't have a good way to answer.

"I will say this much. The discovery of that body led us to find Lynn Dewey. Beyond that—and this is truthful—at the current time we don't know much."

"Have you identified the body?"

"Yes, but don't ask me for information because we have not been able to contact the family. I will say that the identification was made via DNA using the database of the National Council for Missing and Exploited Children. That organization has been extremely helpful in this investigation and were happy to be able to remove Lynn Dewey from the list of the missing."

"What about the people responsible for the kidnapping?" asked a reporter for Channel 11 News who Nathanial recognized from evening news shows.

"Which kidnapping?"

"Lynn Dewey's."

"We don't know how many people were involved in that at this point. As I said, this is still an ongoing investigation. We do know the identity of one person."

Questions were shouted, hands waved in the air. Nathanial held his hand up and waited for them to quiet.

"I will not tell you who that person is but I will tell you that he is dead. No, before you ask, there was no shoot out. The person died in the accident that enabled us to recover Lynn. They were the only people in the vehicle at that time.

"I know you have more questions and I might have answers but I am not going to say anymore that this time. If you will contact my office in Harrisville, we will forward news releases as things permit.

"Thank you."

Nathanial left the room and went to see the Deweys. He walked into Lynn's hospital room and saw the three of them sitting on the bed. They all looked up and Lynn waved at him.

"You certainly are looking better today."

"Yes, mommy and daddy are here. Isn't that great?"

"Yes, it is, Lynn. Mr. Dewey, call me when you are ready to go and we will bring your car to the front of the hospital. There is a state cruiser there; my cruiser will be there also. I don't expect there will be any reporters around but just in case."

As requested, Jim Dewey called Nathanial about 9:15 and at 9:27 the Deweys and a bevy of doting nurses came out the front door. Lynn was buckled into her booster seat, and Mrs. Dewey joined her, sitting behind her husband. Jim thanked all the nurses, shook Mitchell's hand as he had brought the car – him being there was the least Nathanial thought he could do – and then the Deweys headed for Ohio. There were several reporters around but none harassed the Deweys and there were no cameras.

Chapter 38

"Birdshot," exclaimed Nathanial. "Just birdshot!"

"Yes, replied Rich Walker, "and that's all that was in the ammo bag other than shells for the rifle. The shells in shotgun were double-ought but there were just the two. The rifle's a Marlin 30-30, no scope – probably used it for deer. That means he was good but I don't think he was looking to make a stand because the rifle wasn't loaded."

It was late morning and Nathanial was trying to catch up on paperwork after the Dewey's news conference.

"Hmm, what else?"

"The packs just had a change of clothes for each of them and some food. Oh, two thousand in cash, all used bills and basically untraceable.

"We have finger prints of one adult (Williston) and three children. One of them is Lynn Dewey, we compared it with the NCEMC database, and those of Jennifer Duncan, so there was definitely a connection. Still no contact with her relatives?"

"What we've been able to find out is that yesterday was her birthday and they had taken off to get away from it all. Didn't tell the neighbors or anyone else where they were going. Both had two weeks of vacation from their jobs but hadn't told anyone where they were going. Obviously they didn't want to be disturbed. Guess we'll have to wait on that one. Do we know anything about Williston?"

"He grew up in the area, but you knew that. Joined the Army out of high school went to Nam, was there for the last year. It was pretty ugly, his base was almost overrun one night near the end. He was never injured, no medals, clean record. Finished his tour and left. No reserves, nothing. Clean break. Came back to the property his folks had owned near Hibbard Pond and basically disappeared. There is a bank account in Oscoda. His parents left a trust fund he used when needed. Taxes are paid by the firm that looks after the trust. There is no evidence that he has been married nor had any children. Alpena General has no records and we have requests out for other health units in the area.

"On the other hand, as we speak a backhoe is on the way to the site to exhume the two graves there."

Nathanial chimed in, "You've been busy."

Rich Walker chuckled, "We don't mess around, hey, we don't mess around."

Nathanial laughed audibly. "Don't quit your day job."

"Never," said Walker.

"How did you get moving on the graves so quickly?"

"We asked the firm that handles the trust who would have to give permission, and they said that, according to their records, with Williston dead they were in charge and, because of the circumstances gave permission and we got rolling. Strike while that iron is hot."

"Where will the bodies go?"

"Wallace Hibbs is going with us and will take them back to his place in Hibbard Pond. He'll take care of getting them to Blodgett."

"Great, with you guys on the job, I can retire. Anything else?"

"Nope. I guess all you need to do now is to tie up that perch pond body."

"Yes, and that will be no small task."

*****

The town of Hibbard Pond was quiet. The library was closed this afternoon, the post office had no customers, just Owen Whitehawk's SUV in the small parking lot and Wallace's car at the funeral home. Nathanial parked next to it and walked in the back door.

"Wallace," he called out.

"Down here, Nathanial."

There were two coffins in the room, one large and one small. Both contained body bags.

"When did they get here?"

"About half an hour ago. They've both been in the ground a long time – just bones. We lifted the coffins up using a sling on the backhoe. Fortunately the cedar coffins were intact – the planks were an inch and a half thick and this helped. We put them, the caskets, on an air tray ..."

"What's an air tray?" Nathanial asked.

"It's a wood tray we put a casket on to ship on a plane – you just don't ship the casket, at least I don't. I have a couple of them and took them along expecting to need them. Fortunately we didn't need a Zeigler case because I would have to get one from one of the homes in Alpena."

"Zeigler ..."

"I knew you'd ask. It's a metal case we put a casket in to ship overseas – we can weld those to make them airtight. If the bodies had been ripe and the caskets falling apart I would have needed one but somehow I didn't think so.

"I just finished putting the skeletons in these body bags. The cedar coffins are there.," Wallace pointed to the corner. "Rich and Bob, your forensic techs, didn't think they'd be needed as it is just a matter of identification and determining cause of death.

"The coffins, though substantial were crudely made as coffins go. Didn't keep out any of the moisture or other stuff and the bodies weren't embalmed.

"Being in coffins, they are assuming they are not murder victims. Based on the bodies my guess is at least twenty years."

"That means that we will probably know sex and not much else."

"There's DNA. We will know if there was any relationship to Williston."

"Yeah, that would be a start."

"Let me know when you are going to Grand Rapids and I'll send a cruiser with you."

"Will do. I'm going to ask around to see if anyone is going that way like with the perch pond girl. It'll save some money."

"Always glad to help the county's budget," Nathanial said.

Chapter 39

Putting down his pen, Nathanial picked up the phone.
"Sheriff Jefferson."
He had been working for several hours on reports and was proofreading and welcomed the break, however so slight.
"Nathanial, this is Dugal."
"Good morning. What's happening?"
"Not much. I have a question for you."
"Fire."
"Have you identified the girl from the cedar copse?"
Nathanial didn't answer.
"That's okay. I am going to assume by your non-answer that you have but can't say at the present moment. My next question is did she have red hair?"
"I really can't say." Nathanial wanted to tell his friend but couldn't.
"Okay, let's say she does. I would say that her name is Jennifer Duncan."
Nathanial was stunned.
"What would make you say that?"
"I saw Jim Dewey's press conference this morning or at least part of it on the Channel 11 news. I figured that Lynn Dewey was found at Weird Willie's place."
"Again ..."
"I know, ongoing investigation. Anyway, as we have all been doing, I assumed that Lynn Dewey, the girl in the pine copse and the girl in the perch pond are all related.
"Given that, I went to the NCMEC site and did some searching. From reports I knew that the girl in the pine copse was young so I was guessing less than ten years and selected ages 6 -10 years. I figured that Weird Willie ..."
"Let's call him Williston," injected Nathanial.
"Okay. Williston snatched her – and the girl in the perch pond by association – so that she had to be from a surrounding

state: Minnesota, Wisconsin, Illinois, Indiana, Ohio. He could have gone further away but I think that he must have seen them either in the paper or on TV so I was sticking in that area. Also I didn't select Canada because of border security."

"Makes sense."

"I then searched for red-headed girls missing in the past five to seven years."

"Why seven?"

"Well, just as a hunch, Lynn Dewey is three. If there is a connection, then I figured the girls would have been than age."

"Okay, I can buy that," agreed Nathanial.

"I compared the photographs of all these girls with that of Lynn Dewey again assuming that they had to be connected both by red hair and looks and I even narrowed it down by eye color – green - again because they had to look alike."

"You are assuming a lot."

"I agree but let me finish. The only match under those conditions was Jennifer Duncan."

"Lucky there was only one."

"There were three actually. I choose her because she had been in the news prior to her disappearance."

"How's that?"

"She was in that one time beauty pageant which made the Michigan major papers and most television news shows."

"You said major newspapers. What about the Alpena News or Alcona Review."

"I don't know. Can't do that over the web."

"Okay, I'm intrigued. Go on."

"So then I went to the perch pond girl. If she was three when she went missing, that was, from what I know, about twenty-three years ago. I made it twenty to twenty-five. Same state parameters, and I had two that fit. Both still missing. Couldn't be certain. Both had baby pictures and age progression pictures of their current ages, but there are a lot of changes and the two were quite different. So I called the National Center for Missing and Exploited Children, using their tip line. I told them it was a long shot but I think that I knew where one of those two was. I asked if they had an age progression photo from ten years ago for each, and they did. They emailed them to me and I compared them to the photograph of the girl in the perch pond. One was dead on."

"Who?" Nathanial was breathless.

"Norma Miller, missing from Milwaukee. She was a poster girl for foster care adoption."

"We used DNA and searched the NCMEC database."

"But there was no DNA sample. She was a foundling, left in the rest room of a bus station. DNA was so new they didn't take it, is my guess. Never found her mother."

"Norma Miller, you say."

"Yes."

"Interesting, I'll get someone on it."

"Let me know."

"Will do. Thanks, Dugal."

Nathanial put down the receiver and leaned back in this chair. If Dugal was correct – and he was with the first part – the case was just about wrapped up. That would make everyone happy, especially him.

Chapter 40

Two days later, Nathanial held a news conference in one of the garages of his complex. He had scheduled it for the small conference room of his offices but when word had gotten out, the interest shown caused him to move it. As he entered the garage, flashes went off and the huge spot of the TV camera was on him.

"Good morning, glad that you all could be here.

"When we are done here, I am not going to answer any questions. We have a handout for you bearing all the information I am going to give you and more.

"What we know is sketchy and we might never get it much better.

"Nicholas (Nick) Williston grew up in Alcona County near Hibbard Pond. He was in Nam for one tour and returned here after being honorably discharged. While he was in Nam both his parents died in a house fire. Offered grievance leave, he did not accept it. Sometime after he returned he met a woman somewhere, brought her home and they had a child, both of whom died within a couple of years of the birth. They were both buried on his property near his home. We believe this was about twenty years ago. This is because the first abduction that we can attribute to him is that of Norma Miller who went missing from suburban Milwaukee, Wisconsin, June 16, 1991. She was a poster child for foster care and this news was carried on primetime television where it is possible that Williston saw it. Although he lived in the middle of the woods without public utilities, he had a generator and a small television.

"She was playing in the back yard of her foster home. Her foster mother looked out and she was fine, playing in a sand box. The mother went to do something and didn't look out for ten or fifteen minutes. When she did, Norma was gone. No one saw anything. There was never a trace. Norma was a foundling, left in the restroom of a bus station in Milwaukee, most likely she had been born in that restroom. Our guess is that Williston abducted her and drove there and back through the UP but he could have gone through Chicago but there is more traffic and he was more likely to be seen. He may have taken a car ferry over but certainly not back, again because of the people who would see them.

"Norma Miller died on or about August 22, 1999 because that is when Tim Conrad began construction of his dam. She died because of a blow to the back of the head. We don't know whether it was an accident or not and we never will. She was found April 16 of this year when the Hibbard Pond Sportsman were digging a trench through the dam to make a drain down system to be used in rearing perch for eventual planting in Hibbard Pond.

"Two years after Norma Miller's death, on May 22, 2001, Jennifer Duncan was snatched out of a car in the parking lot of a suburban Detroit shopping mall when her mother left her alone for ten minutes because she had fallen asleep and Mrs. Duncan just had to run in to a jewelry store to drop something off. Again no one saw anything and there was no AMBER Alert system in place in Detroit at this time. AMBER Alert was launched in Michigan on June 19, 2001, 28 days too late for Jennifer. No one that was talked to had seen anything and no one came forward. Jennifer Duncan died May 6 of this year in Williston's pickup that went off the Comrock S-curve on East Hibbard Pond Path during a snowstorm. She had the flu and most likely Williston was taking her to the Alpena Hospital but didn't make it. A wheel came off his truck causing the truck to go off the road – this is what he told his friend who came to pull him out. We conjecture that Jennifer died because of the cold when they were trapped there. Of course, like Norma Miller, he couldn't let her body be found, at least not with him, so he buried her in a copse of pine trees wrapped in a blue tarp. We found smudged fingerprints on it that could have been his but were not complete enough to make a certain match. We also found Jennifer Duncan's Tickle Me Elmo doll – this was a week later after we were told about it by Peter Miller, the tow truck driver who pulled Williston's truck out. Williston had thrown it from his truck and it was caught high in a cedar tree and wouldn't have been seen except for the eagle eye of Rich Walker, one of our forensic techs.

"That was enough information to get Jed Parker, Alcona Country Prosecutor, to secure a warrant for the arrest of Williston for suspicion of kidnapping as well as a search warrant from Alcona County Magistrate Judge Judy. We went to Williston property with our warrants and broke the lock on his gate because we had no way of notifying him that we were coming with a warrant. He must have heard us coming because he grabbed Lynn Dewey, whom he called Sue Ellen, and fled in his truck on a forest path he must have cut in anticipation of such an escape. Coming out of a sharp turn he had made in the road, apparently he lost control of the truck and it crashed into an oak. Lynn Dewey was fine, shaken up and scared, maybe even unconscious for a bit because she was not moving when I first saw her. Williston didn't belt himself in and there were no airbags in his old Ford 150. He was thrown into the steering wheel and then out of the truck. He died from his injuries within a few minutes.

"Of course you know the story of Lynn Dewey, kidnapped by Williston from a day care center in Sylvania, Ohio. We believe that he knew of her because of the news of her father's run for the U.S. House of Representatives.

"The obvious question is why did Williston take these girls? Again, and this is only our theory, because they resembled his daughter at the time she died. They were all red heads with green eyes and all taken at about the same age. Whatever the reason, we are glad that we were able to rescue his latest victim.

"We have consulted several psychologists and they have all basically reached the same conclusion. They feel that Williston was suffering from PTSD (Post Traumatic Stress Disorder) most likely, in his case, being either the death of his wife or his daughter. More than likely, they feel, it is the death of his daughter because he kept trying to bring her back. Sadly that is something we will never know.

"Williston was living off a trust he family had left him and has no heirs. We don't know what provisions the trust will make for his property and liquidation of the assets. Honestly that is not our problem. We do know that Williston, his wife if that's what she was, and daughter (this was verified by DNA) will be cremated and buried in the same plot where the coffins for the wife and daughter were discovered.

"Of course, our handout has more information and any further questions should be submitted in writing, emails are fine, to our office.

"Thank you."

As Nathanial headed for the door, one of the reporters shouted out a question. "Sheriff, do you think this will guarantee your election next week?"

Nathanial spun around, arm extended, pointing right at the questioner. "This is about the kidnapping and deaths of two young girls and the kidnapping of a third. It has nothing to do with me."

He turned away and left the room.

Epilogue

"You know, as beautiful as tonight is makes this three hour stint pretty bearable."

Dugal and Earleen were nearing the end of a HPCP patrol. It had become a biweekly event for them although most of them were without incident. During the summer and early autumn they had arranged their nights when the Detroit Tigers were playing on the west coast and the games were late. This entertainment helped to pass the three hours because driving dark roads at moderate speed just isn't very exciting. However once the season – at least for the Tigers – was over, that stopped.

During the early summer months they had taken to looking for deer using a spotlight to spot deer in fields. Usually the giveaway was two green dots shining in the darkness. That had stopped after Dugal had a conversation with Ed Stockwell telling him about the deer count.

"You might want to check on the legality of shining," Ed had said.

And so Dugal had, discovering that they had been guilty of shining as, at least in Michigan, it is not permitted during November or between the hours of 11:00 p.m. and 6:00 a.m. Some poachers – and Dugal thought that anyone who didn't obey the laws deserved to be called a poacher – would shine a light at a deer that always stopped. The old "deer in the headlights" look. Such an animal was then an easy target. Of course, hunting at night was illegal with the legal time being one half-hour before sunrise to one-half hour after sunset.

They had tried books on tape but Dugal found that he was more into paying attention to the story than watching the road and that requires more attentiveness at night than in the daytime. They tried to vary their route as much as things permitted but that wasn't much as there were basically two ways to travel around the lake, clockwise or counterclockwise.

The only excitement they had was coming upon a car pulled over to the side of the road one night. The car had no flashers on and there was no sign of anyone being around so they had notified base and gone on. Patrol rules prohibited them from exiting their vehicle, as that was a job for the police. A cruiser had come and found a note on the windshield saying the owner had run out of gas and gone for help.

Tonight was a night for discussing recent events.

"Glad that Nathanial won the election," Earleen said.

"Yes, I talked to him about it today. He told me that one of the reporters at his press conference about the girls asked if he thought it would help him get elected."

"Gawd, bet he didn't like that."

"You're right there. He said that a count of the absentee ballots had him winning by a wider margin than that of Election Day but it still wasn't close."

"Too bad about that one girl though, the one you found. I am sad about not knowing who she really was."

"We might," Dugal said. "He received a call after the stories hit the press and made national news for one night. A woman in Missouri called and said that she might be Norma's mother because she had left a baby girl in the bus station washroom that night. She was young and couldn't afford to raise it. She is sending a DNA sample so that that her conscience can be more at rest."

"Deer," Earleen said.

"Yes," replied Dugal although he was already braking because he had seen it also.

They were just rounding the first bend of the Comrock's Point S-curve when the beast appeared. *"He was huge, as big as a horse,"* Dugal thought.

"He's huge," Earleen said as though she was reading his thoughts. "Look at those horns."

"They're antlers," Dugal said.

"Okay, mister always right. Horns, antlers, prongs, that's quite a spread."

"I would say sixteen points at least."

"What are points?"

Dugal considered a snappy reply but went with, "I think they mean the number of individual little prongs or tines whatever they call them."

The two of them sat there looking at the stag for a good five-minutes Dugal thought, and then it slowly and seemingly unconcerned finished its passage across the road and into the woods. Just as it reached the edge of the woods, it paused and turned its massive head to look at them. It seemed to shake its head as though saying "yes" and then disappeared. They glimpsed the white tail for a minute and then there was just blackness.

Dugal eased Columbus forward as they looked into the woods for a last glimpse.

"Now's the time I'd like to use that spotlight," Earleen said.

"Me, too," agreed Dugal as he turned his attention back to driving and picked up speed. They went on for another fifteen or twenty minutes, passing their own place and continuing on up to the Leon Creek DNR Launch Site where they had started their evening.

As they turned onto the access road the sky seemed to come alive with light.

"What's that?" Earleen said.

"Don't know," Dugal said.

He pulled the car to a stop in the middle of the parking area, which was deserted because the docks had been pulled the previous week. They got out of Columbus and looked at the northern sky. It was aglow with a pinkish mass of clouds.

"It's almost as though we are seeing the lights of a big city reflected off the clouds," mused Earleen.

"Except there is no big city and the lights of Alpena aren't bright enough to do that. I say it's the Aurora Borealis."

"And you'd be correct," said a voice from behind them.

They both jumped and spun around. Two forms were standing there, feet spread wide and Dugal realized that the two people had bicycles between their legs.

"Sorry, folks. Didn't mean to startle you. I'm Peter Pickard and this is my wife Gert."

"Of course," Earleen breathed relieved, "You own the general store …"

"...and make those great cookies ..." interjected Dugal.

"... and cheese bread," continued Earleen. "We're Earleen and Dugal McBruce and we're just completing our Hic-Cup patrol for the night."

"That explains the pizza delivery sign," Peter jested.

"Good group," Gert answered. "We seen the glow and came out here for the best look at them Northern Lights. This is the darkest place around now that they done turned the lights off for the season. It is so beautiful we decided to ride our bikes."

They all stood there for several minutes looking at Nature's light show, which was starting to fade.

"Don't get them often around here," Peter said. "Conditions have to be just right like tonight. They're one of the many benefits living this far north."

"Are they ever more colorful?" Earleen asked.

"Once in a blue moon," Peter said and turning to Gert. "Guess we had better get home. Someone's got to open the store tomorrow."

"And bake Lemon Crisps," Gert agreed. "Youse stop up tomorrow and I'll give you a free dozen for the start we gave youse and no objections."

That said, she and Peter turn their lights on and peddled off into the night's blackness.

"Guess we better check in with base and sign out," Dugal said.

And they did.

~*~

Meet Our Author

Douglas Ewan Cameron is a retired professor of Mathematics from The University of Akron, Akron, Ohio. He grew up in Oak Ridge, Tennessee, attended Miami University (Oxford. Ohio) and The University of Akron and received his Ph.D. from Virginia Polytechnic Institute and State University (Blacksburg, Virginia). Upon retirement, he and his wife Nancy spend their summers on the shore of Hubbard Lake in the part of Michigan's lower peninsula known as "Up North" and winters in Copley, Ohio. Douglas loves to fish and spends many summer days out on the lake fishing for walleye and smallmouth bass. Retirement has also afforded him and his wife time to travel and they have visited all seven continents. When not traveling or fishing he has been able to return to his writing, something that he was not able to do while working. The stories he writes are those that have occurred to him while either fishing or traveling.

UP NORTH

In Michigan, 'Up North' is not only a geographical region but is also a way of life. Also known as Northern Michigan it is basically the upper half of the Lower Peninsula. The Upper Peninsula (The UP) is not part of 'Up North' but is its own separate entity with its own way of life. The dividing line is usually thought of as a straight line running just north of Flint and Grand Rapids. How far north is debatable as some people say that the line runs through Mt. Pleasant, home of Central Michigan University.

Michiganders enjoy explaining their state's Lower Peninsula to people using the palm side of their right hand. The Up North line described above basically runs across the palm at the base of the fingers. The famous Mackinaw Bridge joining the lower peninsula to the U.P. (upper peninsula) extends north from the tip of the middle finger and Hibbard Pond, where this story takes place, is about a third of the way from the outside edge of the index finger's first knuckle its tip.

Life 'Up North' is slow, easy, and out-of-doors. Michigan is dotted with rivers and lakes and, supposedly, you are never more five (or is it three) miles from a lake, pond, stream or river. To say that everyone who lives 'Up North' is an outdoors person is not totally accurate for there are people who have houses on water but are never in or on the water or in the surrounding woods. But these stories are not about them. These stories are about the people who are truly enjoying what nature has to offer them Up North.

YOUR HELP IS URGENTLY NEEDED

As of February 2012, Tristen Alan Myers was still missing. Below is his picture updated to age fourteen (14). If you think you may know where he is, please contact the NCMEC Hotline 1-800-THE-LOST® (1-800-843-5678). It is available 24 hours a day.

Made in the USA
Lexington, KY
02 January 2017